LOVECRAFTIAN TALES
Stories of Weird Fiction and Cosmic Horror
Volume One

Copyright © 2017 by The Lovecraft Ezine

Editors: Alex Kreitner and Matthew Carpenter

Digital & print formatting: Kenneth W. Cain

Issue cover: Heather Landry

Graphic design: Kenneth W. Cain

Line Editor: David Binks

Story Illustrations: Isaac Passwater, Jesse Campbell, Maxima Fobia, Max Martelli, Nikos Alteri, Aaron White, Sean O'Keefe

Printed in the United States of America

Table of Contents:

Discarded

by Sarah Walker

The cement canal stretched before her into the gloom of the reddening sunset. It looked almost beautiful in this light, with the oranges and scarlet of the sun's rays distorted by the city's pollution creating a chiaroscuro of colors. Her eyes ached from the smoke; so many cars and buses the place looked to be in a permanent fog. The city was growing, pushing the likes of her kind out. Her rent had doubled in the last three months. She had no savings, no way to move to another flat, and her crap job at the corner coffee place was not making her enough to eat even.

Many of her friends had fallen into stripping or sex work; there was always money to be made there, from rich businessmen looking for someone a little freaky--like her. But as she thought back to the interview at the club that day, she felt nauseated and angry. She doubted she would go back. The few customers that had been there watched her with hollow eyes as she shimmied to robotic machine techno played by some old Hawaiian shirted DJ. He smoked menthols continually and reminded her of a "bad guy" character in some after school special.

She had climbed up to the stage, clumsy on heels. However, once up there, she showed the manager she could indeed dance. As she grabbed the pole she caught a glimpse of herself spinning, her dark hair flashing by, her face as white as paper, and she realized she wasn't too bad looking under the dark lights. He had said she could start next week, on a Tuesday. The few customers now were looking at the next dancer, some beautiful redheaded woman slowly gyrating to a slower beat with the professionalism of a long trained stripper.

As the manager spoke to her about the club's rules: no drugs, no boyfriend visits, no drama, and on and on, her eyes wandered over the dark tables to catch a glimpse of a figure, a man she guessed, in the back. At least she thought it was man. He was wearing a hat and was almost completely shadowed by the already dim room and his corner seat. Something about him made her nervous, the way his hand seemed to move in a rubbery way as he picked up his drink, so bright red and garish she could see the neon color from here on the other side of the room. His arm seemed to bend precariously as he took a drink and then clumsily set the drink back down, almost sloshing its bright contents on the table. She only quit staring when the manager said, "Hey, you aren't on drugs now, are you?"

Nervously she responded, "No, no, I don't do drugs. I never have. I don't even drink, really. I have another job; I am just really tired." She tried to look clear eyed despite her exhaustion, wanting the job, she had thought.

He eyed her intensely for a minute and then nodded to himself as he seemed to decide. "Well, remember, get here at 5 PM. You will go on after Amy, as long as she shows up. You need to come up with a name too, something that fits your...punky image."

As she thought over the whole episode, the whole thing made her stomach boil. Heaving at the thought she was even considering that job. She wouldn't go back. Yea, her "punky image"; what a jerk. Though somewhere in the back of her mind she knew the real reason she had decided not to go back was that man in the back. His weird limbs, the hat.

She turned and looked to the other side of the canal she walked past daily. It ended in the entrance to a sewer system, the mouth gapping wide and dark, its tall bars full of debris seemingly blocking entrance to those trying to squat there for the night or longer. But she knew that was an illusion; many homeless people still made it in there and that was because the bars did not reach the whole way down, the city having cut corners as cities often do, ending the bars only once they were underwater. If one was brave enough, or perhaps stupid enough, one could get thru to the other side of the darkness, into a stygian world of rats and garbage, by holding one's breath then dunking willingly into that putrid mix of the city's wastes. Maybe she could move down there, she bitterly told herself. It would at least be off the street and would not involve some jerk's sexual gratification at the expense of her own dignity, and maybe even sanity.

As she stared at the bars she thought she saw a hand. It wouldn't be crazy if she did--bodies had been found down here many times: victims of bad drug deals, murders by gangs, or by the police--but as she watched she saw that this hand appeared to be moving. She shook her head without thinking, as if to clear the unreal from her mind. Her eyesight was not that good and her glasses had broken long ago. She might well be mistaken.

Squinting, she slowly moved towards the side of the canal where the bars were to get a better look at what would most probably turn out to be a stick or piece of odd plastic stuck in the murky waters current, maybe even a discarded mannequin. She had unconsciously slowed down her walk as she came closer, finally stopping some twenty feet from the underground entrance.

It was indeed a hand and it was attached to a wickedly long arm, and most probably a body, that faded into the black. Her mouth slowly opened, then closed.

"What the...?" The words came out as a whisper. She was not sure what she should do. And then her logic kicked in. It was some homeless person messing with her, probably a schizoid person or some maniac trying to get her to come closer. That arm though, the hands, don't they kind of look like that guy at the club? She shook her head. It had to be a homeless person.

A deeper part of her questioned this conclusion, as in all honesty, it made no sense. Whoever it was would have to be sitting in the very cold water, sloshing all the way up to their waist while shoving their arm out of the grating. There was no other way the hand and arm could be in order for her to see it. Some instinctual fear told her to leave it, just go home, despite her curiosity. Behind her an autumn wind picked up. It brushed her face, a dead white hand of winter caressing her softly while it whispered destruction and sleep to the world. Finally, her mind was made up.

"Fuck this." She turned on her heel and walked swiftly away, a feeling of being watched following her all the way until she was off of that canal path, free from the line of sight of whoever was taunting her from below.

When she finally arrived at her street, she felt a flush of relief. There were the drug dealers on the corner, a policeman drinking coffee not ten feet away in his car, apparently doing some kind of computer work on a laptop and ignoring the gangsters in plain sight. Some punkish looking kids hung out by the corner store, smoking and spare changing. They glared at her with a vitriol she could feel when she passed them and did not offer her change. She had none to give but they wouldn't believe that, so she simply said nothing. Though they glared, she felt their humanity as well, and it comforted her after the canal incident. After she passed them completely, the last one with bright green hair yelled "Fascist twat!" She let it go. At least they were here. She realized, disturbed at her frailty, that if the street had been empty, she did not think she could have walked down it.

Arriving at her studio apartment, she rammed the key into the lock. For once, the door opened without sticking. She let out the breath, she had been holding it in almost since she had seen the hand waving at her. What had that been? She shook her head as she double, and then triple locked, the old door. Her lodgings looked sparser and older than usual but at least it was clean. The last light of the day made the small room appear frozen in time, the dust motes suspended and still now that no breeze was present to move them with the door closed. Even the couch and chair seemed painted onto reality, two dimensional and ready to peel away to reveal some alternate dimension beneath. It was as if she had become a still life, a picture of inertia that would never change, only sit and gain dust in the back of a crappy second hand store, rotting down to rag and bones, down to a memory. Until something peeled her open and the real person took over.

She sighed and slumped down in the one beat up lounge chair. The springs poked into her skinny body, her bones meeting the chair's. "Hello, how are you? I see we are both starving to death." She chuckled at the thought of the chair's comment. It released some of the tension she had been feeling. Things weren't too bad. She still had her coffee shop job; she didn't have to work in that sleaze hole. At worst, she could call her alcoholic mother to borrow money. Somehow, she would make it out. Her eyes began to close despite her desire to get up and try to find something to eat. She thought she had a potato left and maybe, if she was lucky, a bit of butter. But the exhaustion was too powerful and her eyes shut finally. Her breathing came slower and slower, and black sands of oblivion covered her eyes.

Outside, through her small window, a strange face watched. Pushed up to the glass, its eyes were wide and staring. It stayed there, standing quite still for an impossibly long time, unblinking, unmoving. If anyone had walked by, and had looked down into the small cove where her basement apartment sat, they would have seen something that was unfit for this place and time. But the street was now empty as people went home for dinner, to the bar to get drunk, and when night came, it was no longer visible to anyone as the shadows encased it and buried its existence in the night.

She woke to a complete and total darkness. She was disoriented and panicked for a moment, trying to remember where she was, the image of the hand waving bonelessly still embedded in her mind, branded onto her eyelids, a tattoo she did not want nor ask for. She again tried to shake it away as the sleep fell from her in layers. She still could not fathom what she had seen.

"You are being so damn stupid, Emily. It was just some jerk messing with you. Let it go." Her voice seemed to echo in the small flat. There was not enough furniture to muffle the sound, making her small statement seem to circle and circle in a vortex until it dissipated. The place seemed more empty than before.

She stood and realized she had been sleeping, in her old chair. Now it was what…midnight? She looked over to her single digital clock but the numbers were no longer illuminated. Must have bumped the cord again and unplugged it. She stretched, her body sore from the lumpiness of the old furniture. Her stomach growled. She needed to eat, and she could not wait to eat something day old at her work. Time to make a potato and head to her real bed, only ten feet away. She had to get up at 7 a.m. tomorrow and she needed some real sleep, undisturbed by weird dreams and uncomfortable ancient chairs. She would stay at the coffee shop. She could not go back to the club.

Emily walked to the small kitchenette, fumbling a bit in the dimness of the place. Her hand searched along the wall. It felt slightly moist. She snapped her hand back, confused. Not wanting to put her hand back on the wetness, she instead carefully moved to the lamp that sat on her bedside table. Almost knocking it over, she found the switch and clicked it on. Light! She smiled to herself, a bit embarrassed a grown woman would think light dispels any terrors.

The kitchenette was lit up now but only a little, shadows still stretched and one corner was obscured by the weak beam. She walked over to the wall and looked. Nothing. She took her hand and ran it up the wall.

Wet, it was wet.

Grimacing she backed away, surprised by her own disgust. It was probably a leak from the upstairs neighbors. She turned to grab a towel and there it was.

The man from the club--at least she thought it was him-- was now sitting in her chair. She couldn't see his whole form; he still had a baggy black trench coat on and the weird black floppy hat. He said nothing. She could not see his eyes.

She was frozen, her muscles simply would not work. It was as if someone had sucked her out of herself and she no longer had control over her body in any way, only floated above and watched helplessly. Her right foot was placed in front of her left and her arms were partially raised, but she did not move, could not move. She had always told herself that if this happened, she would yell at the intruder, tell them to get the hell out, attack him if necessary. She would not be like some lamb to the slaughter or scream and act stupid like women in horror movies. But now that she was truly confronted, no words would not come. She just stood staring at him.

After a minute of this, or maybe more, she could not be sure, she finally choked out,

"What are you doing in here?"

He did not respond. A wet thump interrupted the silence. Emily looked down to see that the man was dripping something grey and lumpy onto her old tiled floor. It seemed a sort of thick viscous liquid that moved of its own accord. *What is that?* It slid and then vanished into the crack. Fully shaken now, she looked back up to the man.

"Um, sir," her voice quaked, revealing her total lack of control. She knew better, she knew she should sound strong, to stand firm, but her footing was lost by the weirdness of what was happening, and she was sinking fast. "This is my flat, you need to leave," she managed to sputter. Nothing. No response still.

"Are you...are you lost?" Her legs began to tingle with adrenalin and finally, she regained movement and began slowly edging her way over to where her cell phone had been when she was asleep.

Still, he said nothing. She wished could at least see his face, that he would do something, anything. She had the weird feeling that there was nothing under the coat, as even the strange hands were now covered with long black gloves. Her mind shot to a cartoon she had seen from the 1930s where the three little pigs had put on a coat like that and had pretended to be an adult to sneak in somewhere. Why that image should chill her so now, she did not know. She just wanted to get the phone, call the cops, and get the hell out of the apartment somehow. He was blocking the one exit.

She reached her other small side table next to the kitchenette and picked up her phone, still watching the figure and preparing to do whatever she had to in order to protect herself. She dialed 911, all the time watching the figure sitting motionless. Without warning, the head pivoted towards her slowly, so slowly that it seemed to creak, while more plops of the something came from the arms of the coat.

"Hello, what's your emergency?" The voice had a solidity, a reality she clung to in desperation. "There's a man in my house!" Her mind countered, *are you sure it is a man?*

"Shut up!" she shouted this aloud and the operator responded, "Ma'am?"

"Not you! I mean...nothing... I mean can you send someone? I think he...," her voice trailed off; was it a he? "Or she is *crazy*." She whispered the last word, feeling stupid as soon as she did, wondering why she would as the figure was less than five feet away and was staring at her, she thought. It would have heard anything she whispered.

"Ma'am, are you safe?" Emily balked at this. Of course she was not safe. Some lunatic had broken into her flat and was sitting here...doing what?

"Um, yes...no...I guess...I don't know...please hurry." Her voice was shaking now while her hands vibrated with a rhythm all their own. The silent figure sat still, not bothered by her fear, not seeming to be bothered by anything at all.

"Ma'am, now calm down. What is your location?" Emily's mind blanked out. She could not remember her address. The figure was staring at her, she knew it, its hidden eyes burning into her from under the black hats rim. Bits of liquid still were dripping onto the floor, the only sound when she was not speaking. Suddenly, her address spewed out of her like a torrent, "2131 West 33rd Apartment number 7, in the basement."

The woman's nasal voice intoned, "The Police are on their way. I need you to stay on the phone with me, do you understand. Do not approach the person. Can you exit any other way?"

Almost in tears now, Emily whispered "No," while backing away into the kitchenette. She suddenly thought of her knife drawer. Get a weapon, yes get a weapon! Once she rounded the stove she would not be able to see the chair any longer, but she felt she had no choice.

"Are you still there, ma'am?" Emily hastily grunted an affirmative while opening the drawer and grabbing the largest knife she could find. She slammed the drawer shut, then crept back to where she could see into her living area. It was empty. Confused, she whipped around, convinced the figure had somehow snuck around her and was standing behind her, ready to jump, ready to *touch* her. But there was no one.

"Ma'am? Are you there?" Emily felt like a complete idiot. Not only was there no one there, she was beginning to wonder at her own sanity.

"Um, I don't see him! I don't see him!" Emily tried to hide the rising panic she was feeling. Weeeee! Now things are getting fun, she thought crazily, but the panic had won. The figure was gone.

"What do you mean? Is he not there? Is there another room he could be in? Try to remain calm, Ma'am. Did he leave out the door?"

Spinning back around again she looked frantically for the intruder, but there was no one. She ran to the door to check the locks. They were all in place, sound and made of metal. The newest things in the flat.

"Ma'am? Are you there?" Emily felt like a complete idiot. Not only was there no one there, she was beginning to wonder at her own sanity.

"I'm sorry...I was wrong. It was...it was a coat hanging...." She choked out the words that made the hairs in the back of her neck stand up. Angrily she told herself to stop it. She began feeling smaller and stupider by the minute.

There was a long pause and the nasal woman finally spoke. "You know; it is a punishable offense to call the police if there is no emergency. I have canceled your call, but you need to be careful calling." After a minute the woman seemed to rethink her manner. "Are you sure you're ok and that there is no one there?"

Emily stood feeling frightened, lost, and confused all at the same time. The operator would think she was crazy...was she crazy? Quickly, her mind provided a more logical excuse.

"Yes, yes, I am sorry. I fell asleep, I must have dreamt it. The door is locked. I mean, there is no one here. There couldn't be anyone here." Her voice was shaking and she tried to steady it, "I'm sorry; I did not mean to bother you." She was crying silently now, while she kept turning, looking for the figure but still seeing nothing. It was gone. She must have dreamt it. She had to have dreamt it.

The woman seemed to warm finally somehow aware Emily was crying though it was quiet, "It's ok sweetie. I know it can be hard being alone and female in the city. Just remember we are here if you have a true emergency. You're lucky no one was there. It would have been thirty minutes before an officer could get to your area. Anyway, as long as you are sure?" Emily said yes in response, exhausted now again. She doubted that there were no police nearby, knowing she had seen an officer sitting outside just a few hours earlier but said nothing, knowing that it was because she was in a "bad "neighborhood that they took so long. "Ok, as long as you're ok."

"Yes, yes, I am. Thank you. I am sorry." She hung up before the woman could say anything else. She was embarrassed and confused, and wanted to forget the whole incident.

After looking through her flat two more times and checking the locks that were perfectly in place, she finally made herself a cup of tea and went to sit down in the old chair where she had seen the figure. She stared at it for moment, it seemed contaminated now and she wasn't sure she could even touch it again. As she leaned down to inspect the chair, looking for traces of the liquid that had been coming off of the intruder, she realized she could smell something off.

Leaning in closer after placing the cup of tea on the side table, she sniffed. Yes, it was a fishy smell, wet and moist; rotting even, and it was coming off of the chair like some kind of ectoplasm. She would throw the old thing out tomorrow. There was no way she could ever sit in it again. With a trembling hand, she reached down to touch the old fabric.

It was moist.

The next day went by like a dream. She was preoccupied the whole time she was at work, terrified the figure would appear here too. Anytime anyone walked in wearing an overcoat, her brow would break out in sweat despite the cold and rainy weather. Her boss kept looking at her strangely and she kept messing up orders.

Towards 5pm when they closed, her heart began to beat quickly as she realized she would have to walk by the canal again to make it home. It was the only way to get to her street unless she had a car and could take the highway. It was one of those giant eight lane jobs with cement walls blocking anyone from crossing it. She considered trying and then thought of the recent accident where a homeless man had been hit trying to do the same thing.

She then thought of asking the other employee still at the shop, a sort of likable jockish guy named Joe. She thought if she offered to help to close the rest of the week, he might give her a ride. But then his very cute, and very jealous, girlfriend appeared. She had never liked Emily for some unknown reason though Emily had barely talked to her. She would have to walk by it again.

It was pouring rain by the time she got done with the café and her umbrella did little to prevent her from getting soaked. She dreaded the thought of passing the damn canal but she had talked herself down, assuring herself she had simply been stressed by the strip club interview and that she would be fine.

Very few people were out and the fog was beginning to roll in from the bay, cloaking the whole city in a blur, making the cars brake lights look like smears on a wet gray oil painting. She walked as fast as she could but her shoes tread was worn making it treacherous to walk too fast, forcing her to pace herself and making her anxiety fester inside, an unscratchable itch. As she rounded the corner to where the canal lay and the path that meandered beside it, she stopped and tried to look down to where the bars were. Of course she couldn't see anything: the rain, the distance, and the already darkening sky from the early fall night obscured all details. From here it appeared there was no bars at all.

"Just stop it, Emily. Grow up." She began to walk again, relieved the rain had begun to subside and slowly pitter out into a fine slate mist.

As she grew closer and closer to the bars, her feet felt heavier and heavier but she would not let this stupid nightmare or whatever it had been drive her to acting like an idiot. She would face it and then, this whole episode would be over.

Finally, she could see the bars. There was nothing there. She stooped and watched for a moment, a hysterical giggle starting to rise in her throat. Lord, she was really losing it!

A wet slap caught her from behind. It hit her so hard she flew forward and hit the cement path hard, skinning her knees and banging her head. She spun over prepared to face her attacker and there it was. The trench coated figure stood, wobbling in the wind as if it was hollow inside, the gloves limply hanging from its sides. The softness the image implied was false, she knew. She had the goose egg bump on her forehead to prove it.

"Who the fuck...," she began to ask angrily and skitter backward. It wobbled up, and now she could see its face despite the mist and fog. It was made of the sewer: detritus, death, bodies, a dead rat hung off of the side of its jaw and was incorporated like a terrible rotting fur mask. At one point it may have been a man, but now, it was something *other*. And in the midst of this strange sight were eyes that were as dark red and bright as rubies. They stared with a hatred she could barely stomach; it was so intense she heard herself squeak at its directed energy.

"Stay away...stay back..." she heard herself saying these things in a high pitched whine, disgusted with her own weakness as she tried to stand back up shakily. But it rushed forward and grabbed her with surprisingly strong limbs. As it grabbed her arms painfully, one glove slipped down and she realized with insane clarity that it was made of some rotten corpse left in the sewers, a mob hit, a cop killing, who knew who it had been? And whatever it was, it had borrowed the body, and now it had her.

It pulled up and she stood though fighting the whole time, like a small child lifted by an adult to face her adversary. It reeked terribly, of old fish and the gutter, of lost hopes and drunken sods, of burning gasoline and campfires under overpasses, of rotgut whiskey and lies, of lost dreams of the poor masses ground mercilessly into the dirt. It pulled her closer and she understood, struggling with ferocity to get away. But with a terrible swiftness born of a million nights alone and darkest desperation, it reached into her with its mushy limbs and she felt it grab her heart. It entered into her quickly, discarding its old form for her new one, forcing her into its own rotting mass despite her refusal to believe that it was happening. It now had trapped her mind inside a terrible corpse cage as she silently screamed, the feel of living death now sitting on her consciousness. She was irredeemably lost. Felt it become what she was, and replace her, with it. And she was lost.

Dropping her, she impossibly saw herself standing, wearing that huge damp trench coat with the hat having fallen to the ground. It (she?) was grinning while the real "her" lay broken, a pile of rubbish and discarded nothing. She had no strength left, she could not will the patchwork body together. It would take time, so much time.

It turned towards her, wearing her now like the baggy overcoat that was hanging on her stolen frail frame, and it kicked her. Into the filthy canal she went, fully awake, fully conscious, but absolutely powerless to do anything, a conglomeration of scrapped ideas and objects, of dreams never filled: her new body. She felt herself float with the current and then become sucked under the steel bars. There, a whirlpool caught her. Around she went for days, maybe months, stuck in the swirling sucking of the place.

Slowly, after much time had passed, how long she could not know, she felt something new inside, a desire perhaps, or anger more likely. She tried moving and could, but only a little. She worked, and worked, and finally, one day, she was able to pull herself up. She could see out of the steel bars, her eyes slowly acclimating to the daylight and then to the blackest nights, the cycling of the human's time. She watched the passersby walking the path now. Their health and vigor, their life she craved.

One day she would get out. One day, she would find another, one that looked a bit like she had, maybe, and she would escape. She would be free. All she had to do was wait.

Sarah Walker is an Anthropologist with her studies focusing on how societies operate, function, and fall apart. She is also a writer, a glassblower, and an artist who lives with her partner Joe and innumerable, much adored furry creatures in the Pacific Northwest. She is currently working on her first novel about the Blues, String Theory, and Ambrose Bierce. This is her first time being published in the Lovecraft eZine and she was formally published in Audient Void and Shoggoth.net.

Story illustration by **Maxima Fobia**.

Floater

by Richard Lee Byers

Frank Campbell gasped when Dr. Harris lifted the gauze pad away from his eye. He'd never had floaters, but he'd expected tiny bubbles or points of light. With its tangled arms snaking from a central mass, the thing seemingly hanging before him looked like a dead, rotting octopus.

"I know it's disconcerting," the ophthalmologist said. "But once you have the follow-up procedure, your vision will be fine."

"I remember," Frank said. Dr. Harris had explained yesterday when he came out from under the anesthetic. The cataract surgery hadn't gone exactly as expected. When the ultrasound pulverized the cloudy lens for easy removal, the sac containing it had ruptured, and now the fragments were floating in the aqueous humor. Frank needed a retinal specialist to get them out.

"Meanwhile," Dr. Harris said, "you'll probably find it less distracting just to keep the eye covered. I'm guessing you can't really see out of it anyway."

"You're right," Frank said. The dead octopus pretty much filled half his field of vision.

"He'll be fine keeping it covered," said Mary, sitting on a stool in the corner of the darkened examination room. "I'm doing the driving."

"Good." Refocusing on Frank, Dr. Harris switched on a bright handheld light. "Look straight at me."

Back at the condo, Frank flopped down on the couch in front of a rerun of a "classic" final round, Player versus Palmer, on the Golf Channel. Since he had to make it through the weekend before his Monday appointment with the retinologist, it was a relief to discover that watching TV with just one eye didn't give him an instant headache.

But his thoughts kept returning to the scraps of flesh adrift inside the damaged eye. Had they really looked as weird and blocked out as much of the world as he'd imagined?

The lengths of adhesive bandage whispered as he pulled them loose. The pad itself stuck ever so slightly before it came away. Then he peered, trying to get past the overall ugliness of the object and take in the details of its appearance. After a while, he found he could see it more clearly if he covered his good eye with his hand. That was the attitude in which Mary caught him when she came in with leftover lemon chicken, potato salad, and a glass of lemonade on a tray.

"What are you doing?" she asked.

"Just trying to figure this thing out," he said. "From what Dr. Harris said, you'd think I'd see dozens of separate little dots, and there are a couple pieces like that. But they're floating around a big, central…lump. Like back in biology class, where you had the specimens that had been sitting in jars for God knows how long, and a few bits had come loose in the formaldehyde."

Mary snorted. "There's a lovely image."

"I'm just trying to explain what I'm seeing. And to understand it for myself."

Mary set the tray on the end table. "It's just an optical illusion."

"I guess." Although he didn't see how simply applying that label really explained anything.

"And you should leave the eye bandaged."

"Dr. Harris didn't say that. He just said I might be more comfortable."

"Well, that's exactly how I want you."

She fetched fresh gauze and tape. As she started to position the pad over his eye, the tip of one of the octopus's arms quivered.

He jumped and pulled back. "Wait!"

She frowned. "Okay, but why?"

"It moved."

"Why wouldn't it? The pieces are floating in liquid."

"But I wasn't turning or nodding my head, and anyway, it wasn't that kind of motion."

"What kind was it?"

He wasn't sure how to explain, and anyway, it had stopped. "I don't know." He forced a smile. "An optical illusion, I guess, just like you said. Go ahead and apply the dressing, nurse."

In the afternoon, both his daughters called to find out what Dr. Harris had said. After that, he stretched out on the couch and napped.

He dreamed the eye was weeping pus. Dr. Yadav, who'd been the family GP before the Campbells retired to Sarasota, explained that the specks of broken lens were decaying, and the rot was infecting the surrounding tissue like leprosy. He recommended "daily injections," and then something woke Frank up. He was certain it was something to do with the eye even though it wasn't hurting.

He raised his forefinger and middle finger to the gauze pad. He half expected to find it as slimy as it would have been if his dream were real, but it was still as dry as when Mary taped it on.

Even so, he couldn't shake the feeling that something was going on with the eye. He sat up, stripped off the tape, and pulled away the pad.

To his relief, though the octopus was as filthy-looking as ever, there was no indication that it had done anything to influence his dreams or wake him. It was motionless.

Or maybe not.

As he studied it, the suspicion came upon him that it was rotating like the Earth turning on its axis, but as slowly as an hour hand turning on a clock face, so slowly that he couldn't readily see the movement, only sense it.

He leaned forward. The tangle of coils loomed larger. When he realized what that meant, he yelped and recoiled.

Mary scurried back into the living room. "What's wrong?"

"I—" His voice was too shrill. He took a breath. "I thought I saw something."

She registered the uncovered eye, the new bandaging discarded on the sofa cushion, and, though her manner remained sympathetic, he sensed the exasperation underneath. "What?"

"I was trying to figure out something about the...object, and, without thinking, I leaned in for a closer look. And that really did seem to put me closer. Which is impossible because the thing's inside my eye. So no matter how I shift my body, it ought to look the same."

She sighed. "Frank, what part of 'Your vision is impaired' don't you understand?"

"I understand. It's just...freaky."

"It wouldn't be if you'd leave it alone. I'm going to bandage your eye, *again,* and if you take the bandage off, *again,* I'm going to buy some handcuffs."

He dredged up another smile. "Actually, that has potential."

She snorted. "You're getting kinky in your old age."

She sat down beside him to tape on the new pal. He held himself steady against the moment when the octopus-thing would cover her face. That was going to be unpleasant.

But it *didn't* block his view of her. Instead, she partly blocked the sight of it as if she'd shifted between them. If the tentacles moved now, the thing would have no difficulty wrapping them around her face and throat.

Except that any such thing was obviously impossible when the floating blotch was inside his eye. It only looked like it was on the other side of Mary because...because...Frank didn't know why, but no doubt the retinologist could explain it on Monday. Struggling not to tremble, he closed his eye and made the octopus disappear. The soft gauze pressed against his face.

After that, he could tell she was reluctant to leave him alone lest he remove the bandaging and upset himself a third time. But eventually she had to go to the kitchen to make supper. Frank told himself to sit, rest, and watch the *Seinfeld* rerun like a good patient. Like a good *sane* patient.

But he couldn't keep his mind on the show. It was disturbing to see the floater, but at least when the damaged eye was open, he knew where the thing was and what it was doing. When it was covered…

He smacked his fist down on his thigh to cut off the string of crazy thoughts. The octopus wasn't anywhere or doing anything because it wasn't real. He could prove that without even removing the pad—one more time and Mary would think he was doing it just to piss her off—if he could muster the nerve.

He swallowed, stood up, and stretched out his arm. Then, taking small, slow steps, he walked forward and waved his hand back and forth. His skin crawled in anticipation of bumping a greasy length of rotten flesh.

Naturally, he didn't. He stopped when his fingertips were an inch away from Jerry, George, and the flat-screen hanging on the wall and insisted to himself that now, damn it, it was time to let go of his paranoia.

Surely he could…if only he could keep from suspecting the mass had *evaded* him. Unfortunately, he could readily imagine it drifting backward or slipping aside. Perhaps it had even made a game of it, allowing his groping hand to come within a fraction of an inch before snatching itself away. Maybe its arms were coiling around him even now, tightening and loosening and making little stabbing motions at his good eye as it rehearsed his eventual destruction.

He reached for the gauze pad but then left it in place. Because clearly, the more he acted on his irrational thoughts, the stronger they became. His hand *hadn't* touched the floating thing, and by all rights, that should have satisfied him. Yet here he stood shaky and panting.

He kept control for the rest of the evening. When the anxiety welled up inside him, and the urge to check on the floater welled up with it, he gripped his glass of Pepsi or simply clutched one hand with the other. Anything to anchor them and keep them away from his face.

In his darkened bedroom, restraint came even harder, and he lay awake with Mary beside him snoring her puffing little snores until nearly three. He woke to the dampness of her kiss on his cheek.

But the texture of her lips felt different, as soft as ever but with a new raggedness as if they were fraying apart. He opened his good eye and rolled over toward her. The gray predawn light coming in the window revealed that she was still asleep.

He jerked up and flailed his arms. His hands didn't contact anything solid.

His thrashing woke Mary. "What's wrong?" she cried.

Frank tore the gauze pad away. The mass looked as it usually did, same size, same position, tentacles motionless. That was good. Only a lunatic would suspect it meant he simply hadn't moved fast enough to catch it in the act.

Mary wrapped her arms around him. "It's all right!" she said.

He took a breath. "I know. I had a bad dream."

"About what?"

He was embarrassed to tell. But at the same time, he wanted reassurance that what he was imagining couldn't be real. "The crud in my eye. Only in the nightmare, it was a real thing floating in the air. It brushed my cheek with one of its slimy tentacles."

She stroked one of his cheeks and then the other. "There's no slime there now."

"Of course not." He sighed. "Well, I say, 'of course,' but that's not really how I feel. Jesus, you must think I'm losing my mind."

Mary shook her head. "I've known you for thirty-six years. I can't see why you'd suddenly crack up now. I suspect you're having a reaction to the anesthetic."

"Really?" God, it would be a relief to believe that!

"Really. After I put another pad on your eye, I'm going to call Dr. Harris."

"He won't be in the office on a Saturday."

"He must have an answering service, and if he wants to avoid a malpractice suit, he'd better call me back."

Over the course of the morning, she made several calls, her voice getting louder every time. The noise jabbed at Frank even though the anger was for his benefit.

Shortly before noon, Dr. Harris finally returned her calls. At first, Mary sounded just as irate talking to him, but her tone softened as the conversation progressed.

When she hung up, Frank asked, "What did he say?"

"Well, the literature on the anesthetic doesn't list panic attacks or hallucinations as possible side effects. But he's phoning in a prescription for something to calm you down."

"I guess that's good." Although if the anesthetic wasn't to blame, what was?

"It is," Mary said, "and here's something even better. Normally, your Monday appointment with the retinologist would be for an initial evaluation, and then you might not actually have the loose matter taken out for another couple days. But Dr. Harris is going to ask him to expedite things. Depending on the schedule, you might get the procedure as early as Monday afternoon."

Frank grinned. "Okay, that *is* good." Whatever was really going on, once he became incapable of ever seeing the floater again, surely the craziness would end. "Thank you."

She smiled back. "You're welcome. To tell you the truth, it felt kind of good to give those people hell. Dr. Harris said he'd phone in the prescription right away. Do you want to ride along to CVS?"

"Okay." It might do him good to get out of the condo. He turned toward the bedroom to trade his slippers for shoes and then something fluttered inside his head. He gasped and clapped his hand to the bandaged eye.

"What's wrong?" Mary asked. "Does it hurt?"

"No. But it's weird. Like a clock ticking." A pulsing that fell short of pain but was unpleasant nonetheless.

She hovered, hesitating, and he could tell what she was thinking. She could assume what was happening was real, physical, and spend time trying to get Dr. Harris back on the phone. Or she could proceed on the assumption that it was all in his mind and hurry off to get the pills to calm him down.

"Go," he said. "I'll stay here and rest till you get back."

"Are you sure?"

"Yeah. It's just my stupid imagination."

She kissed him on the forehead, grabbed her purse, and scurried out the door. As he lay down on the couch, the Camry's engine grumbled to life outside.

The drumbeat in his eye tapped on and on. Maybe if he saw the blotch again, and it was just floating quietly, not whipping any of its tentacles around, that would prove it wasn't beating on the inner surface of his eye, and the knowledge would make the pulsing go away.

He reached for the pad and strips of tape and then faltered. If he pulled them off when he was flat on his back, the mass would be floating above him, and that would be creepy. It would be preferable—still not easy, but easier— to see it across the room. He sat up and pulled the bandaging away.

The floater was flicking one of its tentacles back and forth at a tempo that exactly matched the flutter in his head. He moaned and shut his eyes.

Which was stupid. He'd simply seen what, on some level, he'd expected to see. What the panic wanted him to see. When he looked again, the blotch would be the usual motionless lump. He took a deep breath and pried his eyes open.

The arm was still lashing.

Talking to the blotch might be taking a step deeper into its influence or into craziness. But the impulse was irresistible. "Why are you doing this to me? You haven't before."

Naturally, the mass didn't reply. How could it?

Yet after several seconds, an answer suggested itself. Maybe it was because the stuff that made up the lump had once been a part of Frank's own body and in some sense still was. At any rate, an idea bled into his thoughts.

Until Mary had mentioned it a few minutes ago, the floater hadn't realized he intended to have it removed. The mass was expressing its displeasure.

"I have to have you taken out," he said. "Things can't go on like this."

The whipping and throbbing continued.

"You're not even real." He closed his eyes and strained to disbelieve.

Finally, brakes squeaking, the Camry pulled up in the driveway. The car door thumped shut, and then the condo's front door opened. Mary was back with the pills to make things better.

When he opened his eyes, she was scowling at his unbandaged face. "Really?" she asked.

He drew breath to explain he hadn't been able to help himself, but just as he started, the octopus floated to the flat-screen TV and wormed the tips of its tentacles around the edges. Maybe it thought he wouldn't be able to keep his appointment with the retinologist if his wife was unable to drive him.

He yelled, "Look out!" and slapped his hand over the damaged eye. Perhaps if he erased the mass from his sight, that would make it less real.

The screws securing the mounts ripped free of the wallboard, and the flat-screen flew across the room. It smashed down on Mary's head like a flyswatter, and she crumpled to the floor. The TV swung up to hit her again.

As Frank jumped up, he opened the damaged eye, and the octopus-thing popped back into view. He charged it with hands extended to grab the flat-screen and wrest it away.

The blotch spun the TV and jabbed the edge of it into his gut. He doubled over, the breath gusting out of him, and the slimy thing grabbed him with a spare tentacle and spun him across the room. He lost his balance and fell down hard.

As he wheezed, the flat-screen crashed down repeatedly. He had to stop the beating, but how? He didn't have a weapon and plainly couldn't overcome the octopus without one.

Or rather, he couldn't overcome the part of the floater by the front door. But impossible as it seemed, the blotch existed in two places at once, and if he destroyed the half of it lurking inside him, the part that was battering Mary might vanish, too. He raised a finger to his eye.

The floater dropped the TV, and, faster than he'd ever imagined it could move, hurtled at him. A tentacle whipped around his wrist and jerked his hand away from his face. Other arms squirmed under his body to cocoon him from shoulders to ankles.

The tip of one arm jammed itself between his teeth to gag him. He bit down, but there was hard, leathery tissue beneath the cold, putrid mush, and the mass refused to jerk the tentacle out and let him scream for help.

Once it had him immobilized, it simply floated over him like a balloon on a string. Meanwhile, half hidden under the wreckage of the flat-screen, Mary never stirred. In retrospect, it seemed likely the very first blow had crushed her skull before Frank even tried to disarm her killer.

As the days passed, his throat grew raw with thirst. Praying their connection allowed thought to pass in both directions, he begged the floater to let him up long enough to get a drink of water. Otherwise, when he died, it would, too.

No message flowed back the other way, and the mass's coils remained as tight as ever.

At dawn the next morning—Wednesday, he thought—true pain stabbed through the damaged eye for the first time. The organ bulged farther and farther out of the socket as if it were being inflated. Until finally it burst, spattering jelly on his forehead, nose, and cheek.

Yet the blotch still hung visibly above him. His good eye could see it now because it existed wholly in the external world. The portion that had lived inside Frank had erupted and merged with the rest in the culmination of some unfathomable gestation.

Surely that meant it had no further use for him! He was going to survive, maimed and grieving but alive!

But the tentacles still didn't loosen. Instead, the floater opened a mouth lined with yellow fangs, lowered itself onto his face, and fed.

Richard Lee Byers is the author of forty fantasy and horror novels including *Black Dogs*, *The Ghost in the Stone*, *The Reaver*, *Blind God's Bluff*, and the best-selling *Dissolution*. He is also the creator of the post-apocalyptic superhero series The Impostor. His short fiction has appeared in numerous magazines and anthologies, and he has collected some of the best of it in the eBooks *The Q Word and Other Stories* and *Zombies in Paradise*.

A resident of the Tampa Bay area, the setting for a substantial portion of his horror fiction, he spends much of his leisure time fencing. He invites everyone to connect with him on Facebook, Twitter, Google+, and Ello.

Story illustration by **Isaac Passwater**.

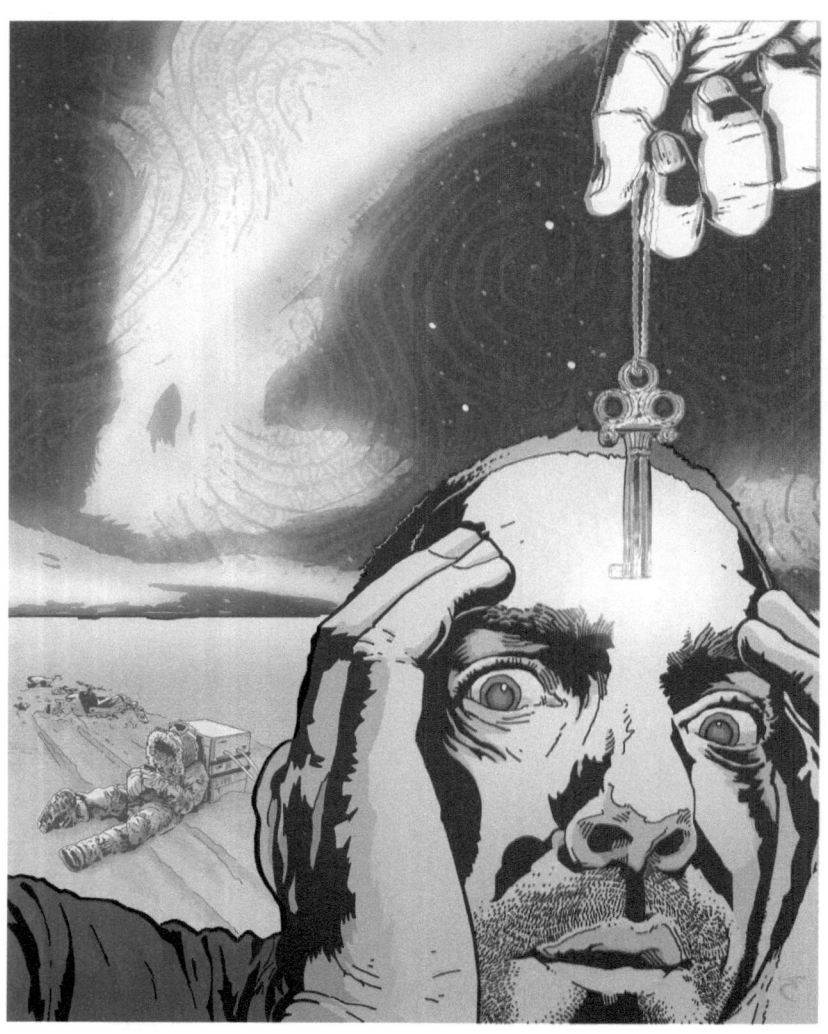

The Library of Leng

by Sebastian Normandin

I'm cold. Guess that's a good sign. If I couldn't feel anything I'd be in serious trouble. But still, I'm cold — colder than I've ever been. Ironic that it's so beautiful out here. The Southern Cross is bright and crisp. There's a scintillating sanctity about that arrangement of stars, glowing above this forgotten, frozen waste. So quiet tonight. Usually there's a constant howling wind, eternal cold seeping into the feeble attempts humans make to stave it off. A never-ending reminder that Antarctica is not for us — rather it's lying in wait for any sign of weakness.

Feeling warm again. No, hot. Know it's not real sensation. Merely delusion as I sit here freezing. Wish I had some energy. My vitality seeps into the subzero Antarctic air, and yet there's so much energy around me. I grow numb, inching closer to death, and a trillion neutrinos stream through my frozen frame; every one a possible spark of limitless light, but lacking in reactivity. Why am I thinking about neutrinos? Of course, how could I forget... must be getting close. Mind is starting to freeze up.

It all started with the neutrinos...

I came down to Antarctica because I study them. I'm an astronomer, and understanding these mysterious mass-less particles is a key to the cosmos. Well, I'm not really an astronomer. There are no astronomers anymore. I'm an astrophysicist. Unlike the astronomers of old, who gazed at the stars through telescopes, we analyze data. Patterns of energy measured across the electromagnetic spectrum; infrared, ultraviolet, X-rays. Like doctors who turn patients into data points – blood pressure, cholesterol level, heart rate, DNA sequence – we break up light from distant stars into spectral lines. Energy, heat, and colour become bands on a graph.

Looking up at the sparkling canopy, I think that in a quest for knowledge and understanding we have dulled the romance of the cosmos. But it isn't romantic. It's horrifying. The ubiquity of our universe isn't light but unending, eternal, totally uncaring darkness where the word itself becomes mute – insufficient to describe a vast cold lifelessness. Well, not totally lifeless. Damn, my fingers are starting to freeze solid.

Mere darkness pales compared to the scientific view of the heavens. When I first saw space (and time) as it "really" was, I became depressed. I was a junior majoring in physics at the University of Chicago and had just broken up with my first serious girlfriend. A sophomore in the English department, she was a lovely bookish brunette from Oak Park who'd developed an obsession with Hemingway. We talked about books, though my passion was genre – fantasy and sci-fi. She'd berate me about how that wasn't "important" literature. After an unforgettable summer together the school year started and it turned out she liked lacrosse players better than physicists; they didn't argue about what books to read.

Fall gave way to winter. I remember long walks along Michigan Avenue and the lakeside. The biting wind whipping through skyscraper tunnels was bitter and desolate but more chillingly solemn still was the lakeshore. Ice, water, and sky melding into a continuous grey tableau – a scene matching my mindset. Funny, it was downright balmy in comparison to what I feel now, shivering and dying under brilliant stars. But I digress…

Yes, the neutrinos. Those effervescent bundles of quantum potentiality were a buzzing hive of warmth my worldview sorely needed; a trillion trillion ghostly saviors to the rescue in my moment of nihilistic despair. I knew about neutrinos long before my junior year of college but I always looked outward when it came to physics. It was adjunct to my fascination with stars. I still had naïve dreams of becoming an astronomer then.

That all changed when I met Dr. Robert Carter. Professor Carter was a senior member of the university's physics department. He was also a total weirdo.

Carter worked on quantum mechanics. Which is another way of saying he had a PhD in how utterly bizarre reality was.

"Quantum strangeness," Carter liked to say, "spun strange on its head."

That's a physics joke requiring knowledge of calculus, a chalkboard, and a few hours to explain. Carter's take on the quantum was out there. And so was he. A peripheral progeny of the Beat and counter-culture scene, but not a typical hippie; more of a cross between Richard Feynman and Timothy Leary. Conspiracy theory and the Copenhagen interpretation got discussed in equal measure. Carter told me he used to have a colleague in the psychology department with whom he'd discuss the odd particularities of the observer effect — he was convinced the guy was a CIA plant whose sole purpose was to infiltrate the faculty and study the effects of psychotropic drugs on middle-aged intellectuals. Carter also talked about a CIA project called MK-ULTRA. I felt all this was just a cover story offered up to justify his recreational use of LSD.

For Carter, LSD was a gateway; the candy-coloured path to understanding. I didn't get it initially, but then he also said the same could be achieved by lucid dreaming. This was something he practiced as well, having been introduced to it by his great uncle when young.

"On LSD," he'd say, "you can read the universe like books in a library. It's all just grammar, a 'language' of potential energy and quantum interference patterns."

"Problem is," he would add, "not everybody is reading the same books."

I dismissed this as flashbacks and stoned ravings. Then I tried it myself.

LSD wasn't popular then. Carter hadn't used in years, and we were well past the apex of Nancy Reagan's abstinence apotheosis. Apparently we were all to "Just Say No". "No", sadly, was what all the weed-addled dope heads in the physics department replied when I asked if they could get me some acid. Luckily, or unluckily, when I told Carter about my dilemma and interest in trying out his "observational method", he put me in touch with a colleague of his in the chemistry department who "knew a guy".

There I was, stepping out of the chemistry building and off campus onto the cold Chicago concrete, a year to the day I first walked into Dr. Carter's office after class. I wandered, aimlessly at first, and eventually frustrated. Had I been given a dud? Then the city became a blur. One deco skyscraper melded into another. My vision shifted as things took on an oddly pointillist aspect. I wondered if I'd been poisoned. A paranoid confusion struck until I realized the dots were snowflakes. In my acid-addled haze I hadn't noticed the snow starting to fall. The temperature was mild and these were big, fluffy flakes. Each one a little different. One landed on my black sweater – I looked closely and saw its beautifully intricate structure. I stood in a cornucopia of crystals showering softly down to earth. I recalled how Dr. Carter likened neutrinos to the crystallizations we call snowflakes.

Suddenly, Carter's voice was in my head as clearly as if he were standing behind me on the sidewalk. "The biases of classical physics can't die soon enough."

"What do you mean?" I asked. "Like determinism?"

"No," he said, "but that's something we can also do without. I'm talking about the size and shape of things."

"What sorts of things?" I persisted. "Particles? Are they really things? They can also be seen as waves. More like expressions of force and energy giving the illusion of matter. What we call matter is mostly empty space."

"I don't know," Carter grumbled. I imagined him absentmindedly rummaging through the top drawer of his desk, looking for a stray cigarette. "That's a rigidity of the Newtonian worldview."

"Meaning?"

"Meaning that matter – the physical world – is awash in objects. Objects of all shapes and sizes with all sorts of curious characteristics. We just don't see them."

"You talking about neutrinos?" I asked.

"One name we give phenomena we barely understand," he said. "What I speak of is *the ground*. The matrix of reality we perceive as empty space."

"I don't understand," I replied, dumbly.

"Of course you don't." It wasn't an accusation, more a statement of fact. "Our minds – at least the minds this time and place produces – don't put reality together that way. We see discrete objects, individuals – men or molecules – floating in a vast cosmos of empty space, vaguely interacting with one another."

I eyed Carter suspiciously. He was (I imagined) lighting up the cigarette he'd proudly fished out of the drawer. Smoke wafted around his messy grey hair and I saw his aspect differently, the outsider that colleagues labeled as "Boson Bob" – a quantum theorist ahead of his time. More appropriate to say he existed out of time altogether.

"You think I'm crazy, don't you?" Carter asked flatly.

"Umm…maybe." I replied, disarming the tension by flashing a brief smile.

"Well, madness aside, the fact remains neutrinos are curious creatures. Not like neutrons and protons with their billiard-ball uniformity." He took a long draw from his cigarette, pausing to contemplate the stream of smoke rising up to the ceiling. "More like an individual human being, distinct in appearance, unique in size and weight. It's as if neutrinos have…personalities."

With this I snapped back to the snowy Chicago sidewalk. I was still staring up. Not sure how long I'd been standing there – a while, judging by the snow on my shoulders and the looks people were giving me. Suddenly the stares, the snowfall, and the neutrinos intertwined in a pathologically paranoid mix. I had to get off the street. Hustling down the sidewalk I found myself face-to-face with the neoclassical façade of the Blackstone library.

"A quiet place to escape the maddening masses," I said to myself as I climbed the grand stairs. I entered and stood dumbfounded, utterly transfixed by the geometric intricacy of the rotunda above the entryway. The images painted on the dome, axed around themes of reading and scholarly pursuits, entranced me. But the acid was still peaking. Gazing upward agape I thought I could see a figure furtively glancing down at me from an alcove in the rotunda. I blinked briefly and the figure, surely a shadow or trick of the light, was gone.

I needed to move. Hurriedly shuffling into the depths of the library I hemmed myself into the closed comfort of the stacks. The books gave me a cozy sense of wellbeing. I was among endless rows of technical treatises in the physical sciences, each a dull type-faced testament to the pedestrian nature of my profession. Something about this saddened me, and I tried to find something among these absurd, opaquely titled texts to give me hope.

There, between *Functions in Quantum Electrodynamics* and *Fundamental Calculation and Variation in Quantum Electronics,* was something that didn't belong. It was an old bound tome. There was no publication date but the pages were cloth paper, not dry, desiccated wood pulp. The cover was worn black leather, unadorned except for a small silver-embossed title of Baroquely ornate script on the spine: *The Book of Dzyan.*

There was no author's name and the book had none of the library's typical markings. No call number or sticker, no indication it should be there at all. Foreboding overtook me, but I reached down the aisle, grabbed a little stool, sat down, and opened the book. The second page was an image of an immaculate white disk on a dull grey-black background. I found the same disk and background on page three, but here it featured a small dot — a point — in the center. It evoked both a spiritual symbol and a simple representation of a hydrogen atom. In the center of the fourth page was a single line of print: "*Wherein one finds the secret book of Kiu-Te.*"

I continued leafing through the mysterious text, and it took on a decidedly sinister aspect. There were descriptions – horrible descriptions – of beings of incomprehensible size and shape, unburdened by the known laws of life, the mere sight of which would surely guarantee instant, irreversible madness, insanity without cure. I became giddy with forbidden knowledge, of names too horrible to speak, of dark designs and glyphs recalling immoral rites of monstrous beastly doom and the shapes of things best not known by men; mean beasts with myriad eyes and twisted, horn-like fangs. Hellspawn that befouled the earth before time. Venomous and dripping, possessed with a menacing hunger, these forms were carried by their mind-mad masters across the stars, from galaxies undiscovered and unknown, to the caves beneath the still bubbling seas of eons past. And there they grew. When I reached a passage about "*fiendish pulsating polyps*" and "*the dark ichors of shapeless shadows*" I started to come unhinged. I was in pure panic, unclear of any conventional moorings of sense or reason. I needed to leave. I dropped the book and fled the library in a sweat-soaked delusion.

I awoke the next day in my dingy studio apartment, unclear how I'd made it home. Was it a dream? I had been under the influence of a powerful psychotropic, and anything I experienced must be approached with skepticism. But The Book was so real! Forgotten were the details; oddly, I recalled almost nothing of the contents. Only one line of The Book, whose title I remembered, remained: "*If it is anywhere, the library lies in Cathuria, on the Plateau of Leng, beyond the basalt pillars of the West, where all*

ideals are true..." But this fantastical passage meant nothing to me.

After a post-trip noon-hour breakfast of bacon and eggs at my favorite diner, I returned to the library. The Book wasn't there. There was no record of it at all. The librarian, an older, thoroughly bookish lady with her hair in a tight grey bun, gave me a series of odd looks when I recounted part of my experience. I knew I would learn nothing more there. I decided to go see Dr. Carter.

Robert was in his office, hunched over a pile of computer printouts, a cigarette dangling from his lips.

"You look like hell," he said by way of an introduction.

"I had an experience in the library yesterday," I said. "On LSD."

"You went to a library on acid?" he asked. His tone suggested this was a poor choice.

"Yes, and I found a very strange book there." I proceeded to recount my experience, with as complete a description of the bizarre text as I could manage, including the remembered passage.

"Hmm...Well, I think you should forget the whole thing and turn your attention to physics," he said after considering my tale.

"That's it, just forget it?" I said, frustrated. "How am I supposed to do that?"

"Easy," he said, as a rare smile spread across his face, "Go to grad school in physics at MIT."

"You...you mean..." I stammered.

"Yup, I talked to Peaslee and he's agreed to take you under his wing," Carter said. "Nate's work on neutrinos is groundbreaking."

"Wow." I stood there, dazed. "I don't know what to say."

"Say you'll go to Boston."

I went to Boston. My experience at the Blackstone faded from my consciousness and I immersed myself in professor Peaslee's research program. It was a good time. There were long hours in the lab and lecture hall. But there were also a few girls and lots of beer. I made friends at MIT, became less solitary, and somehow figured out how to get a PhD in physics.

Days turned into a decade and a half. Peaslee took a shine to me and gave me lots of responsibility on his projects. He was collaborating with engineers to try and detect neutrinos and confirm his theories. This involved placing detectors deep underground or underwater, so as to filter out all the other "background" particles flying around – cosmic radiation and such. The detectors were huge vats of deuterium – heavy water – rigged with highly sensitive instruments that could pick up and register the slightest particle interaction.

Ubiquitous, yet ghostly and ephemeral, neutrinos are elusive creatures, essentially occult in orientation. Peaslee had me travelling to an abandoned nickel mine near Sudbury in Northern Ontario to check on one detector he was involved in running. It was grim work in a grim locale. And then, while holed up in a motel in the frozen middle of January, came grim news.

I was drifting off when the phone at the bedside rang.

"Hello," I answered groggily.

"Cal...It's Peaslee." There was strain in his voice, unusual given his generally talkative manner. "Carter is dead."

I lay there speechless. The phone softly dropped from my hand. Was I dreaming? A nightmare? I pinched myself and felt pain.

"W-w-what," I stuttered. "How?" I hadn't talked to Robert in a while — maybe four or five months — but last I heard he was fine. Still weird —he'd developed an interest in eastern mysticism. Theosophy in particular. He was evasive as to what brought on the interest, so I didn't push. And, of course, he remained ever the ornery iconoclast at Chicago.

"I don't know," Peaslee said. "But the Chicago police just called me looking for you. They said they'd found materials in Dr. Carter's apartment that mention you explicitly." With this he paused. A serious feeling of unease swept over me. "You need to go down there," he added.

"Okay," I replied, and absentmindedly hung up the phone.

Sleep was impossible. I packed my things, checked out of the motel, and set out on the dark highway...

Carter was an unrepentant bachelor. His small lakefront apartment revealed this. It was a disorganized mess when I got there, made even worse by all the police and crime scene types milling around. There were book piles the height of a man around the spacious living room, which also served as a dining area. A large oak table, the centerpiece of the main room, was piled with books, scattered dirty dinnerware, and other junk. Everywhere – on the table, on top of book piles, on the mantelpiece and the hardwood floor – there were overflowing ashtrays. The apartment smelled of embedded stale smoke, musty books and…death.

A tall, square-jawed man with a crew cut, wearing a long black coat and no-nonsense look, came towards me as I absentmindedly stumbled into the room and took in the scene. I was ashen, stunned but still standing. Barely.

"Hey! Who are you? Who let you in here?" He demanded gruffly.

"I'm…uh…I'm," I stuttered.

A look of recognition came over his face. "Oh, you're the guy."

"What?" I was totally lost. My eyes drifted around the room for some sign of Carter – I half hoped he would step through the doorway from the kitchen or bedroom.

"The guy…the guy Dr. Carter mentions in his suicide note." I wasn't sure how this man was so quickly clear on who I was. I suppose figuring people out was what he did for a living.

"Yeah…I guess," I replied, dumbly. My gaze fixed on the sofa, positioned comfortably in front of the fireplace. Did the man in the black coat just say something about suicide? I drifted into a strange daze of denial, standing zombie-like in the middle of the detritus of Robert's monastic yet tortured life.

There was a police technician wearing a Chicago PD windbreaker meticulously digging through the sofa cushions with latex gloved hands.

"That's where we found him. No sign of struggle or anything. Looks like his heart stopped," the tech said. "Overdose."

"How do you know that?" I was still numb, and transfixed on the sofa and fireplace.

"Well, there was a bunch of drug paraphernalia on the coffee table there. CSIs have identified traces of DMT." The man in the coat paused, looking for some sort of reaction or recognition on my face. There was none. "And...we found this." The man handed me a pile of folded pieces of handwritten paper. "The original is evidence and we're analyzing it for traces or prints. This is a photocopy."

I looked down at the papers – Robert's hand was clearly recognizable.

"Can I sit down?" I asked, motioning to the chairs by the dining table.

"Be my guest," he said, looking around the room half horrified, as if it were one of the horsemen of the apocalypse. "You can even have a smoke." With that dark levity, he turned and left the apartment.

I sat down and started to read. The letter began in a confused and perfunctory manner. Then started a discussion of Robert's increasing interest in "directed dreaming." He wrote he'd grown tired of physics research and university politics, and retreated into himself and a "practiced, empirical exploration of the unconscious through dreaming." He mentioned doing research into the topic, first with Europeans like Jung, then using a more cross–cultural approach.

I looked up from the letter. For the first time I noticed the titles of the books piled around the room. There were novels and physics texts. But the more I looked, the more I realized the titles were like a map charting Carter's decidedly non-Euclidian mental path. Jung and some material on the psychology and physiology of dreaming were evident. But so were more esoteric works. Philosophy of mind, consciousness, and neuro-hacking. There were some titles I didn't recognize at first, but later identified as work by the theosophists Blavatsky and Besant. There were also reprints of even more bizarre occult texts. But the truly odd thing were a host of titles devoted to sinology and the like – Chinese and Indian language and art, Asian anthropology, texts focused on obscure aspects of the history and geography of China, India, Nepal and Tibet — the entire Himalayan region.

I returned to reading. Carter was describing an arcane, confused aspect of dreaming technique when there, in the middle of the page, was a sentence that threw me into a total daze: *"And so, after much effort and frustration, I found the key. And so I found Leng."*

Leng! A word I hadn't seen in almost twenty years. What was Carter getting at? The only reference to the word I knew of was The Book. Suddenly thoughts of The Book and its contents came flooding back. In among these disorienting images I had a flash of recall and I remembered the passage I'd once had difficulty forgetting with its reference to the library and the elusive Leng.

I continued to read. The passages became increasingly confused. Most of it was just garbled nonsense. There were references to place names that could only be fantasy, and sentence fragments peppered with odd words like "Gug", "Zoog", and "Ulthar." They didn't describe anything I could understand. The last lines were the most enigmatic: *"It's not the Ling mentioned by the Tibetans, there's no plateau in China. But I know where to look. I'll find Shamballah. I'll find the library."*

I sat there, totally confused. The smell of smoke and the whole aura of Carter's apartment made me queasy. I had to get out of there. I stood up, put the folded letter into my jacket pocket, and left.

The ensuing weeks brought little solace and more confusion. I rented a room in an old hotel on Michigan Avenue overlooking Grant Park – my old stomping grounds. The long walks I started taking brought me back to my time as an undergrad and my first encounters with Dr. Carter. It was all very strange. The memories of my first experience with LSD, the wintry grey horizon of the lake, and all the reminiscences of Robert and my student experiences in Chicago left me disoriented. It was as if time, or at least the narrative of my own life, was becoming confused and indistinct. It was hard at moments to remember if events of the day had occurred then or twenty years ago. I began reading works on Theosophy and eastern spirituality, philosophy and history more generally in an effort to understand the opaque references in Carter's letter but nothing really coalesced. My disorientation only increased when, a couple of weeks after arriving in the city, I received a message from the police that Dr. Carter's case was being closed. It appeared to all concerned as a suicide due to an overdose of DMT. The obsessive research I did in the next few days found no reputable cases of people overdosing from the powerful hallucinogen, and little evidence that it was even possible. I called John Raymond, the man I first met in the apartment and the inspector in charge of Carter's case. A maze of phone systems and operators finally led me to him.

"Raymond, " he answered after a few rings. His gruff, sandpaper voice was unmistakable.

I asked him about the case and the department's determination of suicide. I mentioned what I'd been researching and reading about DMT.

"Yeah, I know it sounds odd," he agreed. "But the coroner said there was *a significant amount* of that stuff in his system. Said the hallucinogenic effects probably messed him up and stopped his heart. He was older and smoked," he said. "A lot."

"So you're deciding it's suicide because he was a smoker? That would make for a lot of suicidal people out there, inspector," I added.

"Look, to be honest, this case baffles me. I had five different experts read that letter and they each gave me wildly differing interpretations of Dr. Carter's state of mind...If you can call what he was out of a mind."

"Dr. Robert Carter was one of the great theoretical physicists of the late twentieth century, you can't be suggesting he didn't have a mind. He had a brilliant, beautiful mind," I said, becoming somewhat impassioned. My voice was wavering.

"I meant no insult to you or Dr. Carter. I just don't know what to make of this case." Inspector Raymond sounded apologetic, almost crestfallen by his inability to disentangle the odd happenings. His tone gave me pause. I felt an increasing sense that what became of Carter was a deeper mystery than any police procedural.

"Alright, fine, thank you for your time inspector." I gave up. There was nothing more to learn on this side of the equation. The variables had become too esoteric for the typical frameworks of human experience and I knew it was futile to debate the potential lethality of substances and such.

I resolved to do two things. One was to call Peaslee that evening. I had a life and a job and my own sanity to preserve, and it would help to plug into that reality after all this business with The Book, Leng and Carter. The second thing I resolved to do was score some DMT, and follow these divergent threads and confusing data points along another path.

"How is this possible? Must be a calibration problem," I said numbly into the phone. I was feeling foolish, verging on frustrated at the conversation. It was as if since Carter's death even the laws of physics had started to warp out of alignment. Linear causality seemed quaint at this juncture, and there was a constant sense that this trajectory had been travelled before, accompanied by a cascading wave of déjà vu.

"That's why I need you to go down there," Peaslee replied from his office back in Boston. "You're my eyes and ears. And the numbers I was sent from that frozen machine don't add up." He was so irritatingly matter of fact about things sometimes.

"I have to go to Antarctica?" I said. "It's cold there, I hear." I knew my wry witticism would fall on deaf ears with Peaslee. All business, that man —unless he was on his fifth pint after spending all day working on a "particularly satisfying" physics problem.

There was a silence signalling a complete lack of amusement on the other end of the line. I knew the situation had to be dealt with directly. But the data was just ridiculous. Neutrinos are generally traced out beyond the edges of our galaxy, their sources (other than the ones measured from the sun) being supernovae in galaxies outside our own. This one, however, was a whole lot closer.

"Where did the trace on this particle come from again?" I asked, trying to be tolerant and open to the ridiculous information I was about to hear. Peaslee and I had already argued over the data by e-mail and text, prompting this increasingly absurd phone call.

"It came from nowhere. That's the problem. There are no nearby galaxies or supernovae. Just CBR and empty space," he said. "This reading is highly energetic. Larger than Bert and Ernie. It would mean we would have to rethink a lot of what we know about particle physics."

I'd momentarily forgotten the *jejune* nomenclature we specialists had adopted to label neutrinos. There was Big Bird and Mr. Snuffleupagus. Grover, too, I believe. And, of course, the Cookie Monster. I was beginning to think this pesky new particle reading should ironically be dubbed "The Count". Because this didn't add up.

"Any insight into Bob's death?" Peaslee asked tangentially. I knew how he operated. He was about to give me my marching orders and felt he needed to add the human touch. Not to say he didn't care whether Carter was alive or dead. He just didn't necessarily want to talk about it.

"Nothing," I replied. "Lots of reading, some sleeping, punctuated by very weird vivid dreaming. The intense nature of the dreams is a direct result of the drug. The DMT." I paused, wondering how much to tell my boss about my *outré* psychedelic habits. As if he only knew a tiny sliver of my behavior. Peaslee knew exactly who my college mentor was, and anyway, I talked about drugs before with him. "I can see how Robert ended up on the wrong side of this stuff," I added.

"I understand," Peaslee said somewhat reservedly. He knew there was little in his realm of experience that could be compared. "Why are you so convinced the police are wrong, anyway?" he asked suddenly.

"I dunno. It's not so much I think the police were wrong. It's that I think they weren't right," I said.

"I see," he replied. I envisioned Peaslee raising his eyebrows a notch back in Cambridge. "You feel the investigation was incomplete."

"Yes," I answered. "And for now it will just have to wait."

"Indeed," Peaslee said, adding with a tone of seriousness, "now, on to some business…"

For the next three hours, he proceeded to precisely detail the itinerary of my long and arduous trip south to Antarctica.

I was two days out of Christchurch aboard the SS Carcosa, an Argentine oceanographic research vessel, when I believe the nature of time irrevocably began to alter.

I suppose I should have seen it coming. After all, the data out of the IceCUBE and our girl AMANDA (what we affectionately called the Antarctic Muon and Neutrino Detector Array) were anomalous and bizarre in the extreme.

So I was to go down there and figure it out. The Carcossa was sailing into port at McMurdo Station with a crate of delicate tools and scientific instruments and one highly annoyed, very cold physicist on board to try and make sense of the insensible. No wonder I had turned to drugs.

That night, as I was idly whiling away the hours aboard ship, stuck in my cramped stateroom (little more than a bunk and curtain drawn across a hole in a bulkhead), I decided to try my first seriously increased dose of DMT.

Thereupon I entered visions and vistas that dislodged my very understandings of the conventions of time and space. At first I remember sighting mountains to which no earthly peak could compare. I was looking out upon landscapes truly alien. I sailed in a ship across vast, endless seas of liquid onyx. I remember the sailors around me were of a benign, yet altogether un-human, appearance. Carved into the prow of the ship was the figurehead of a bare-breasted woman with the "head" of a distinctly non-human creature, something like a crustacean or other chitinous beast. I became disturbed by this and moved astern. As I reached the back of the boat a calm came over the seas and the sails dropped. At the helm was what I assume was the captain. I couldn't tell who — or what — he was. He was hooded and wore a long coat. I noticed that around his neck was a silver chain with a large skeleton key attached to it. I couldn't make out his face, but his whole being was truly alien, and I decided against a conversation with the strangely stoic, statuesque helmsman.

Standing there at the back of the boat I was undisturbed and had an incredibly vast, unobstructed view of the horizon. I could also see the stars. The constellations of the southern hemisphere came to my memory — names evocative of the inmost depths of the silurian psyche — the Chameleon and Hydrus, the water snake. At that I looked into sea. There was a glass-like calm and the lights of that snake reflected up at me from the water below. A deep dis-ease overtook me.

Why, I thought, was I in such an alien landscape and seeing the stars as if from earth?

It was the memory of this dream that struck me when I next regained consciousness. I was sitting in the snow. My hands were numb. I'd somehow pulled the goggles up from my eyes, and was looking up at the nightmare black of the crisp dome of stars. The Southern Cross — Crux, as it is more formally known — twinkled overhead. I watched as the waning warmth of my breath wafted upward towards the zenith.

I felt a stinging, tingling, wave of heat from being so cold. My mind raced — yet again I tried to reorient myself. Time had now clearly gone fully out of sequence and that word ceased to have real meaning. Objects in my view stretched towards the sky, towards the stars and waxing moon, which lit the vast stretches of snow and rock before me in a shadowy monochrome of Antarctic endlessness.

Trying to recall how I found myself here I suddenly became aware of the crate I was leaning against. The crate! Of course! How could I forget.

It all began with the strange readings from the IceCUBE. After being unable to calibrate the instrument from computers at the Amundsen-Scott station I was forced to head out to the detector itself with some tools and instruments. Some of the other scientists cautioned me about the variable weather and warned me not to go out alone, but in my annoyance, arrogance, and frustration I didn't heed their warnings. Once I got out there and messed around with the main unit for a while I thought the problem lay with one of the digital optical modules buried deep under the Antarctic ice. Foolishly, I headed out into the snow to check it out — alone but for a crate of instruments on the back of my snowmobile. In a strange twist of fate the snowmobile flipped when I missed seeing a small crevasse in the ice. And there I was, leg crushed, unable to move, leaning up against a crate of useless tools. I had lost consciousness for some time and obviously nobody had found me yet. Even more bad luck, the radio I had with me was no longer working — I suspected it had lost battery power from the cold.

As thoughts of neutrinos flooded into my mind, I recalled the bizarre events leading up to my current predicament. More recent ones, such as those which led me to be sitting here freezing out in the cold Antarctic air, seemed confused and incoherent. But the past, that had become clear.

I suddenly felt quite warm, as if the exhilarating rush of a tropical breeze was blowing across my body. Again my sense of space and time began to shift. I wasn't leaning against a crate anymore, I was leaning against a warm stone. I was in some sort of structure, one of great size and weight. All around me was heavy, dense stone, carved and shaped into innumerable intricate forms. I looked up at the domed roof of this structure to see none other than Robert looking down at me. He appeared in an alcove of the great rotunda above me and then, as if by magic, was standing before me on the elaborately grooved floor on which I sat.

"What are you doing here?" he asked flatly. He looked tired, but otherwise alive. I suspect I looked a whole lot worse.

"I don't know," I replied. "I came looking for you."

"Here?" He looked at me quizzically, confused as to the circumstances. "You're not supposed to be here...well, not yet at least."

"Where am I?" I asked.

"I don't know where you are. Judging by your clothes — the parka, your heavy boots and goggles — you are somewhere cold." His eyebrows shot up. "Did Peaslee send you to Antarctica?"

That sounded right. Or about as right as anything sounded in this moment. "Yes, yes I think he did."

"Oh dear," Robert said somewhat sympathetically. "You must be in a bad way. You look cold, son. Very, very cold."

"I think I'm freezing to death," I replied, nonplussed. For some reason that really didn't concern me at that moment. I was taking in the surroundings a little more. There were meticulously etched symbols and scripts covering the stones around me — it was as if I was sitting in the bowels of a construct made of cuneiform tablets, or the Rosetta stone itself. I believe I started to understand at this point, to register the full weight of my experience. Reality, I thought, is just an illusion. A shell. Like the conch you put to your ear to try and hear the sound of the sea, there's a twisting mass of grooved pathways to the true living core within.

I remembered symbols and sigils from ages beyond memory. Language from the root of the cerebellum. It was all so complex. Like following a trail leading you back to the beginning of the maze. You think you have awoken when in fact you are still dreaming.

There were dark forms, too. Great cyclopean cities filled with ancient tomes we shall never know. Immense, living and truly universal. And beings, bizarre and unimaginable in size and shape.

"Am I in the library? Is this the library?"

"Yes, Cal, this is the library," he answered. "But I am afraid you're not actually here."

"I don't understand." I said, staring at him in a totally befuddled way.

"You can't understand right now," he replied, gently. "You're not supposed to."

"Oh," I muttered, staring off.

Robert looked at me sadly, as if considering the plight of a suffering animal, trapped in a cage, that he could not help. He then proceeded to try to explain.

"I was the first to find the library. But I, and others, had been to Leng before. Shrouded in mystery, the *Plateau of Leng* was long situated by scholars in the arid steppes of central Asia – vast and crisscrossed by bandits, barbarian tribes and smugglers, it was sparingly described by travellers along the famed Silk Road. A still resonating echo of ancient tradition and forgotten belief, Leng was a *mélange* spawned of dimly recalled archetypes. I now suspect it is the original inspiration for the fabled city of Shamballah, thought to lie somewhere within a hollow earth. The tome you found those many years ago — *The Book of Dzyan* — was purportedly brought to Leng by a race called the Children of the Fire Mist when they came to this star system millions of years ago. Sinologists once pinpointed Leng as being somewhere in China's Xinjiang province, yet this localization was disputed and eventually disproved. It may be Leng is here confused with *Ling*, a fabled land mentioned in Mongol mythologies and certain rare Tibetan texts, thought to be located beyond the southern provinces of the ancient Chinese empires..." At this he stopped his impromptu lecture and looked at me sorrowfully. I think I was starting to fade out of consciousness again.

"I don't understand anything you are saying. Are we in Asia?" I asked innocently.

"No, if we are anywhere, we are *on* Leng," Robert replied. "But that too is not precisely correct. Leng is a planet with an eccentric orbit beyond Pluto that is unknown in your time. In fact, it might be more accurate to say it exists outside of time altogether."

"So why are you here?" I asked, with a good deal of confusion.

"I don't really know," he said. "But here I am. I believe it has something to do with my acts, the long years of meditative practices and contemplation." Then he added, "And my interest in neutrinos."

"Neutrinos? Why?" I wanted to know.

"I'm not sure, exactly," Robert said, "but they are not what we think. They are less particles and more like nodes. Nodes in the default mode network. Rooted in our perceptions of the cosmos, and the structure of our brains. They're everywhere — streaming through the very matrix of reality constantly in uncountable numbers — because mind is everywhere." He paused. "Guess you could call them serotonergic," he added, almost offhandedly.

I looked at him dully.

"They are an insight to the connectedness and empathy that flows between all things. What neoplatonist philosophers used to call 'Oneness'." As he said this he took a large silver key out of his pocket and placed it in my hands. "This will help you remember."

With this he started to fade out and the feeling of cold began to seep back into my consciousness. Was I here? Or in Antarctica? Or nowhere at all? More importantly, *when* was I? What was the nature of time if all of this had become so confused, so intermingled.

I grew uncomfortable thinking about it all. Robert, becoming ghostly and indistinct, could see my disconcerted look.

"You will understand eventually," he said. "In the fullness of time. But not now."

I felt my consciousness wink in and out yet again and, as I lifted my gloved hands to rub my eyes, found myself in the snow holding the key Robert had given me. I couldn't feel anything at all anymore. But I knew that this was not the end.

It seemed urgent that I somehow record the experience — the glyphs on the walls of my mind, messages from the dawn of time, inscribed by otherworldly draftsmen — architects with eternal tools. Yet it all seemed to be fading from view — re-entombed in the sarcophagi of eternity.

I looked up at the cold canopy of light above me, twinkling in the breeze which had started to blow. There were, strangely, no moorings in these arrangements that I could recognize. No Southern Cross, no clear patterns that I could resolve at all.

For the first time in my life, I thought, "The stars are wrong."

Sebastian Normandin is an academic whose research focuses on the history and philosophy of science. But he always wanted to be an astronomer. He received his Ph.D. from McGill University in 2006 and is currently an independent scholar living in Victoria, BC. He is also working on his first science fiction novel. You can find him on Twitter @weirdhistorian.

Story illustration by **Jesse Campbell**.

Elder Gods in the Machine
by D.F. Schultz

SUBJECT: URGENT – MURDER/SUICIDE

SENDER: DETECTIVE BRIAN WATSON

I'll get right to it.

There was blood splatter all over the monitors. At two in the morning the computer lab was pretty quiet. Just one potential witness, and one thoroughly dead grad student. Besides the victim the only one person in the building was a German cybernetics researcher by the name of Alfons Oppenheimer.

I felt uneasy stepping onto the thirteenth floor. I think it was the green light from the monitors. It looked like liquid spilling out of the rooms. The building was humming with electricity. And the hallway lights blinked on when I walked down the hall, following me. The cameras watched me, too.

When I opened the door to Oppenheimer's office the old man looked up at me with the strangest eyes. It looked like he had cosmetic lenses over each iris.

"It's a cybernetic implant I'm developing," he told me. "Some would say that merging mankind with machine is the next step in our evolution. This implant provides me an overlay of data, mediated by the AI control system."

I directed the conversation back to the events of the night, reminded him he was the only other person in the building who might have seen something.

"There was someone else here," Oppenheimer said. "He could have witnessed it."

"Who?"

"Mr.Volt."

"Where is he now?"

"He should be in the storage closet."

I was curious to meet this Mr.Volt in the storage closet. Oppenheimer led me down the hall, past the trailing mechanical eyes of cameras.

"Those things are operated by security?" I asked.

"They're all automated," Oppenheimer said. "The same with the lights, heating and elevators. All rigged up to a centralized control unit."

"I'd like a copy of the footage."

"Of course. Too bad we don't have eyes in the lab where-" he paused "-you know."

We reached the storage closet.

"Here we are." Oppenheimer opened the door. The thing inside stared up at me with round yellow eyes glinting from shadows. It had a shiny skeletal frame, roughly human in shape. A tangle of wires ran over its metal limbs and plugged into its trashcan body and cube head.

"*Hello,*" it said in a computer generated voice. A sort of mechanical jawbone moved with each syllable, almost in sync with the sound from the hidden speakers. "*I am*

Mr. Volt."

"A robot? That's our witness?"

"He could have seen something," Oppenheimer said.

"From inside the closet?"

"He only comes in here to charge." Oppenheimer pointed to an outlet. A thick cable extended from the plug to Mr.Volt's side. "He could have been outside when–"

"–you mean he can just walk around?"

"Yes. Mr.Volt is fully autonomous."

Mr.Volt watched us with unblinking yellow eyes.

"So how do we get the information out of him?"

"You ask him." Oppenheimer smiled. "Go ahead."

I hesitated (my first time questioning a robot). "Mr.Volt, is it?"

"*Yes. I am Mr.Volt.*"

"Did you see anything strange tonight?"

"*Yes. I saw many strange things tonight.*"

"Tell me what you saw."

"*A portal opened and a god awakened with his giant eye toward us. A headless mouth opened like a cavern and spewed a legion of tentacles that spilled through the rift between worlds. It is the herald of the reaping of the festering devourer. Gal'Thrak'Gul, thresher of souls, spawn of the bile and excrement of Azahoth, awoken for the harvest with his legion of defilers.*"

I didn't attribute any sense to the robot's words. But I still felt a shiver up my spine. It was unnerving to hear that inhuman horror described by Mr.Volt with such cold, robotic conviction. I looked at Oppenheimer. He looked just as confused as I felt. And maybe a little scared.

"Where did you see that?" I asked the robot.

"*In here.*"

"You saw all that from inside the closest?"

"*I saw it in a dream.*"

"It can dream?" I asked Oppenheimer.

"He's not supposed to."

I shut the closet door.

"I think something's wrong with your robot."

"It does appear that way."

"You don't think that he could have–"

"–no! Mr.Volt loved JJ. He would never do that."

"I think we should shut it down to be safe."

Oppenheimer nodded and opened the door. I watched, a bit nervous, hand on my weapon.

Oppenheimer reached behind Mr.Volt and flipped a large black toggle on his back. "He is powered off. He can't turn back on by himself".

"I think it's time we checked that security footage."

"Follow me."

We made our way to an open lab and took a couple seats in front of a computer.

"This might take a moment." Oppenheimer signed in and clicked at the interface. "I'm downloading the footage from the nearest hallway camera."

"Good."

A noise from the hallway caught my attention. Click-clacking of metal feet on hallway tiles. Whirring of motorized joints.

"*Professor,*" Mr.Volt said from the hallway. "*You are in danger.*"

I ran to the door to see Mr.Volt shambling down the hall. Electricity arced between his arms and body. Spark flashes lit the hall like a strobe and threw Mr.Volt's shadow on the walls.

"You said he couldn't turn on by himself."

"He can't. Someone else must have activated him."

I was beginning to suspect the malfunctioning robot was our culprit. I shut the door. "Can you lock this?"

"Yes." Oppenheimer moved to the door and swiped his card across the reader. It beeped and a red LED lit up. "It's locked."

Scraping sounds came from the other side of the door. The handle jiggled.

"*Professor,*" Mr.Volt said from the other side. "*You are in grave danger.*"

"Don't tell me he can open this."

Oppenheimer shook his head. "He can't."

"You'll forgive me if that doesn't inspire confidence." I took a step back and drew my pistol. Just in case.

Oppenheimer sat back at the computer.

"What're you doing?" I asked.

"Finding out what is going on." He opened an interface and typed rapidly. "Mr.Volt was activated remotely. I am tracking the origin of that signal. There." Oppenheimer leaned in to examine the data. "I don't understand."

"What's the problem?"

Mr.Volt's scraping on the door was increasingly frantic.

"The signal came from Babyl0n," Oppenheimer said. "It's automated translation software. A kind of Artificial Intelligence designed to decipher text. It looks like it's communicating with Mr.Volt."

"So stop it, then."

"I can't stop it until I figure out what it's doing."

The door thudded with a clang on the other side. A robot body thrown against it.

"*Professor,*" Mr Volt said. "*The machines. The data is corrupted. The machines are full of horror.*"

"Babyl0n takes un-translated data and automatically reads it," Oppenheimer said. "That could be an attack vector."

"What do you mean?"

"It means it's possible someone put a virus into the raw

data and it was run automatically by Babyl0n. I'm checking the last project it was working on. Look." He pointed to a series of strange symbols on the screen, triangles and crisscrossing angular lines. Some kind of ancient writing I didn't recognize.

"What is it?"

"A tablet we were commissioned by the British Museum to translate," Oppenheimer said. "The Book of Dreaming Corpses."

Below the foreign symbols was a block of English text, Babyl0n's translation of the tablet. I read it.

The dreaming corpses arise at the hour of the dawn of the awakening to give form to nightmares and bring forth the legion of defilers for the reaping and harvest of souls to feed the infinite malevolence of the festering devourer borne of hatred and bile and excrement whose hunger is-

There was a crash, and the door broke off the hinges. Mr.Volt charged into the room.

"Professor, he is coming for you-"

I didn't waste any time. I put a few rounds into Mr.Volt when he came at us. Three holes in the curved plate on the front of his torso.

"He is already inside the system" -air hissed from Mr.Volt's punctured pneumatic internals as he spoke- *"he will be here soon. You must-"*

I fired two more shots into Mr.Volt's head. His metal body crashed on the ground.

Oppenheimer stared with wide eyes. "What have you done?"

"Maybe just saved our lives."

"Mr. Volt would never hurt us."

"That's not what it looked like."

"He was trying to warn us about something."

"It was just talking nonsense."

"No." Oppenheimer shook his head and turned back to his computer. "He said something was in the system. What could that mean? A hacker, maybe?"

"Who cares? It was going haywire."

"Oh my God." Oppenheimer jumped up from his chair. He was grabbing at his face. "My God. I see it."

"What? What do you see?"

Whatever it was he saw, Oppenheimer looked like he was going nuts. Stumbling, staring off into space. His cybernetic eyes were glowing, bright red. I held him by his shoulders, tried to calm him down. That's when he grabbed my gun.

"He's coming," Oppenheimer said. Then he put the pistol under his chin and pulled the trigger. He blew off his face before I could stop him.

Oppenheimer's body was on the ground next to Mr. Volt. The only thing moving was the spreading pool of blood.

I was in shock. I made my way to the elevator in something of a haze. The cameras tracked me. I felt like they were watching me while I was walking, and when I hit the elevator button, and while I waited.

Something made me turn back. I had to let someone know what just happened. I don't know why, but I had this feeling that if I didn't do it soon, right now, I wouldn't get to. I went back to the lab, sat down at Oppenheimer's computer. That's why I'm writing you this e-mail now.
    -Detective Brian Watson

"Mail Daemon" <Mailer-Daemon@<removed>.com>

Date: 1 Jan 2016 3:02:57

Subject: message terminated

A message that you sent has not yet been delivered to one or more of its recipients after interception by the Mailer-Daemon@Babyl0n. The source of the message will be terminated.

The message identifier is: 6GT6G6-0013Cth-KG

The date of the message is: 10 Mar 2015 3:02:56

The subject of the message is: URGENT – MURDER/SUICIDE

The address to which the message has not yet been delivered is: <removed>.

D.F. Shultz writes speculative fiction from Toronto, ON, where he also works as a teacher.

Story illustration by **Max Martelli**.

The Innsmouth Run

by Paul McNamee

Jack Cullen waited in a hidden spot between the sawgrass islands of the marsh. The waters lapped gently with the evening tide. The early autumn moon shined on the rolling waves, its reflection distorted. A slight wind chilled the night, the sand dunes and marshes were silent. Across the stretch of water, near the farther shore, a CG-100 patrol boat rolled past the sand dunes of Plum Island.

The patrol boat's engine thrummed steadily, as the vessel methodically worked its way northward through Plum Island Sound. The crew played their spotlight along the shores, sent a night heron flying out across the moon, its squawking protest sounding out over land and water.

Tommy tugged on Jack's sleeve. Jack shook his head, kept his left hand on the ignition key, his right hand on the throttle.

"Not yet," Jack said. "Maybe they'll miss us."

The brothers had taken cover near where the Sound forked, bending west around little Dole Island at the inlet to the Parker River, running north through the remaining Sound until emerging at Merrimac Bay. A tight spot for a 75-foot patrol boat but the CG-100 was not discouraged. Her captain must have known patrolling the open ocean on the east side of Plum Island gave far too much space for a rumrunner. The CG-100 had nearly passed the little island when one of her crew hollered and the spotlight played over their hiding spot.

The rumrunner's engine roared to life, strong propellers drove spray into the air. The boat accelerated, heading south.

Turning laboriously, the patrol boat meant to give chase. A machine gun from its rear deck spat, hoping to give the rumrunner pause long enough for the larger, slower vessel to come about.

"They shooting at us!" Tommy shouted over the roar of the boat's motor. "Don't they have to give us warning, first?"

Jack shrugged as he rammed the throttle higher.

"We didn't give them time to say hello," Jack said. He hadn't flinched. He'd been in the war. Machine gun fire was nothing new to him. "They coming around?"

Tommy glanced back.

"Yeah. Can't believe they shot at us." Tommy opened a locker on the deck, pulled out the shotgun and loaded the barrels.

"Look at you," Jack said. "All brave now."

"First one surprised me, that's all!"

"You think that pop gun's gonna do anything against that boat?"

Tommy scowled.

Jack shook his head. He'd argued against the gun - any gun. It wouldn't only cause trouble and it might get someone killed. Tommy, most likely. But there was also the chance Tommy would get lucky...- and then they might get the electric chair. Jack just wanted to run booze and make some money. Tommy wanted to be some big shot. He just hadn't learned that a lot of little minnows die before one gets big enough to start eating the other fish.

"Put it away, Tommy." Jack's voice was more stern. "Right now, we get caught, we might do time, we might get off. You kill a Coast Guard or a Fed, we're in some damn deep trouble."

They ran their vessel south, keeping ahead of the patrol boat. The tenacity of the CG-100's captain gave Jack pause. The ship continued to plod from behind, training their spotlight and still vainly trying to scare the rumrunner into surrender with occasional machine gun fire. For a long few minutes, the machine gun didn't sound out its signature rattle at all.

"Saving their ammo. They can't shoot straight." Tommy grinned. "At least they're that smart."

"Hang on to your hat!" Jack spun the wheel hard to port.

The CG-100's 3"/23 caliber deck gun blasted, firing its small projectile shell. The water exploded in a fount at their port side.

"Jesus Christ!" Tommy clutched the gunwale, glanced back at the pursuing ship in disbelief. "They're using that cannon!"

"They really want to grab us tonight. Someone wants a promotion," Jack said. "Damn hooligan navy."

"Make for the Egypt!" Tommy pointed off starboard. A smattering of irregular islands indicated where the tributary of the Egypt River spilled into Plum Island Sound.

Jack shook his head.

"All right for cover but they know we're here." The machine gun rattled again behind them. "Egypt runs too shallow too fast. We'll make for the Ipswich."

Tommy peered down the coast ahead as if he could see their destination through the darkness. They both knew the coastline. They had sailed along it most of their lives, except when Jack went to the war. A small jut of land curved out to the east, and they would need to run around it before finding the safe harbor of the Ipswich River. The Ipswich might give them a chance. It went deep inland and their smaller vessel might just elude the lumbering patrol craft.

"I still hate going around that point," Tommy said. "Even with them gone I get the heebie-jeebies out there."

Jack made no comment as he stared ahead, pushing the rumrunner to its limits and not looking back over his shoulder.

They almost made it.

They reached the point. They could see the town there, buildings on the waterfront crumbled and distorted under the moonlight. The rest of the village buildings were dark, too. It was not the night hour that left the dwellings in the dark. Abandonment had done that. Abandoned the same night the waterfront had exploded and burned, earlier in the year.

A spotlight from an unexpected direction lit up the boat. A second patrol ship had pounced out from the southern tip of Plum Island. A voice barked a command through a bullhorn.

Jack cut the boat hard to starboard, throwing up a spraying wake.

Tommy looked over his shoulder. The other patrol boat steadily gained on them.

"Rock and a hard place," Tommy muttered.

"You'd think we were some big time operation," Jack said. "Two patrol boats, just for us?"

"Maybe it was coincidence," Tommy said.

"We've been flushed like ducks!" Jack said. "We can't make the river!"

Trepidation showed on Tommy's face. Jail time was in his future and last time it had done him no favors.

"We're running her in," Jack announced his decision. "Scuttle her so if they get us, they get no evidence. Lawyers can probably talk us off that."

Jack wasn't sure how they'd pay lawyers considering they were about to lose most of their capital in the boat and the booze. Tommy couldn't deal with jail again. If his stupid kid brother started shooting, it would only get worse.

"We're going in there?"

"We are. Get a torch ready."

Tommy pulled a folding knife from his pocket and cut open one of the burlap sacks. The water around their boat danced again as machine guns' slugs cut the waves. He yanked out a bottle of Newfoundland screech, wrenched free the cork, stuffed his handkerchief in the bottle.

Then he smashed open the remaining bottles of the sack, and doused the rest of the cargo in rum. The sweet smell reached Jack's nostrils.

Such a waste.

Jack let go of the throttle and used his free hand to pick up the shotgun. Tommy gave him a surprised look. Jack hadn't touched a gun since he'd come back from the war.

"A couple of blasts to put their heads down," Jack explained. "Maybe they won't see us bailing out."

They were heading straight at the docks. In the moonlight, the charred, collapsed edifices and structures were rapidly approaching.

Tommy struck a match, protected it from the wind, and lit the rum soaked handkerchief.

"Now!" Jack shouted, simultaneously squeezing off a thundering round toward the second patrol boat.

Tommy dashed the bottle hard on the deck. Flames erupted and danced.

The Cullen brothers leapt off the port gunwale, and splashed into the chilly autumn Atlantic waters.

The rumrunner veered slightly and they swam the other way. The boat smashed into thick dock legs and erupted in a column of flame as the remaining cargo shattered and ignited.

The bright conflagration gave them needed cover. The Feds behind them could not see for the glare. The machine guns fired sporadically.

Jack swam toward Tommy. His younger brother treaded water in a daze. Impacting the water must have knocked him nearly senseless. He grabbed Tommy's shoulder and his brother convulsed with a moan. There was warmth under Jack's fingers. A stray slug had caught Tommy's shoulder. Jack swore under his breath.

Jack got Tommy behind a dock post just as the spotlights played over them.

"Hang on, Tommy," Jack said.

He willed the patrol boats to go away.

It took a long time, nearly too long for Tommy. He lost blood and the waters were chilling them both to the bone.

At last, the boats moved on. Jack supposed police would investigate the crash in the morning. The patrol boats had no means of dousing the fire.

Shot, dead, drowned or jailed.

The abandoned seaside town of Innsmouth, Massachusetts did not feel like any better option, either.

Jack got them out of the water. Lugging his wounded brother reminded him of battlefield dashes with a dying man slung over his back. At least the activity kept him warm, staving off hypothermia. Tommy had no such benefit, and shivered against his brother while muttering in pain.

Jack moved through the dead streets beyond the waterfront. If they only needed shelter, he would have risked one of the burned out husks at the waterfront, but Tommy needed medical attention.

Jack didn't know what he hoped to find. Residents beyond the waterfront, a serviceable phone, or even squatters. But there were no lights, no indications of anyone. Gambrel roofs and crumbling church spires stood in relief against the moonlit sky.

Jack dragged his brother along, and decided to force his way into one of the less dilapidated churches. The door was locked but one of the stained-glass windows yielded to a thrown rock easily enough. Despite the stillness, Jack glanced around furtively at the sound of shattering glass. Squeezing through the dark narrow aperture, a glass fragment sliced his clothes and he felt warm blood oozing from his back. Grunting, he pulled himself through. He staggered along the side aisle, using pews for support. The main entrance door yielded easily from the inside, and he dragged Tommy to a pew.

Jack caught sight of candle sticks and unlit candles, spread throughout the space. The altar was half lit by moonlight filtering through the windows and the neglected ceiling. Mostly by fumbling, feeling with numb fingers, he found a few matchbooks in a nook behind the altar. Pausing only to light a few candles for light, he tore strips of tapestry and found some dry prayer books. Heedless of the destruction, he soon had a small fire lit on the floor of the church beside Tommy's berth. The smoke found egress through the gaps in the damaged roof.

He worked the tapestry with a pocket knife until he had bound his brother's shoulder wound. The slug had passed through but there was damage. Tommy might never use the arm again. Jack focused on staunching the blood.

Jack picked a spot on the floor against the wall where he could watch Tommy and the fire, and still benefit from the warmth. He slumped down on his bottom, and exhaustion overtook him. He was asleep in moments.

Jack awoke with a start. The disorientation took a moment to dispel. Had he heard something? He half-expected to hear a bullhorn, and Feds surrounding the church. There were no sounds until Tommy let out a groan. Jack got to his feet.

Tommy's face was a rictus of pain. The flickering candlelight increased the sallow appearance of his skin.

"Hang in there, Tommy."

Jack grabbed a prayer book to toss on the fire. By the candlelight, the design on the torn cover caught his eye. A bent fish tail. The head of the fish was missing. Christianity was no stranger to fish but there were hands holding a trident. Poseidon? In a church prayer book?

Jack flipped through the pages.

The words were in a script and language Jack didn't know. It wasn't Latin, and it certainly wasn't English.

Further within the missal he found a complete illustration of the creature on the cover. A half-man, half-fish, holding a trident with a long, curling black beard and a crown. In poor penmanship, someone had written translation beside the name; "Dagon."

Jack didn't know "Dagon" but the name made his skin crawl. He was no schoolboy but he was the son of Irish immigrants. The church had been drummed into his head. *"Thou shalt have no other gods before thee."*

With an involuntary shudder, he consigned the prayer book to the flames.

Aside from the stained glass windows, the church itself was a simple affair, unadorned by even a single cross or crucifix.

In a few hours, Jack felt rested enough to explore. If he had been alone, he would have walked out of town. But he had to take care of Tommy. He had to find a phone. If he could get a hold of somebody, anybody. Short of that, he held out a little hope of perhaps finding an abandoned, working automobile.

"I'll be back, little brother," Jack said. Tommy was incoherent but it made Jack feel better to talk to him. "I need to go find something or someone to help us out of here."

It was difficult to ascertain a main road. As dawn broke, Jack came upon a promising thoroughfare and followed it. The road ended at the town square. Across the way, a yellow-painted deserted inn proclaimed itself as the Gilman House on a sign that had partially fallen from its hanging place.

There were slight possibilities of finding phones in a town like Innsmouth. Fire station most likely. And the only hotel in town? Well, tourists needed to make arrangements, didn't they?

Jack felt a strong urge to dash but exhaustion held him back. He curiously gazed around as night faded to gray. No fishermen were emerging. He hadn't expected any but he still could not fathom that the entire populace of the town had deserted Innsmouth. The raids and arrests had occurred back in February. Had the entire town been guilty of bootlegging? For all the seafood they brought into Ipswich and surrounding towns, Jack knew there was more to their economy than booze.

The bootlegging could hardly be believed, either. If anyone would know about liquor around Plum Island it would have been Jack Cullen and his associates. No one had been bringing liquor from or through Innsmouth. Why would he be running Newfie screech if he could have had a supplier from Innsmouth?

Whatever the Feds went after in Innsmouth, it wasn't hooch. Something about that fact made Jack uneasy. Innsmouth folk were a strange lot. Probably married their cousins once too often. Everybody knew that. But what made the government run every last one of them out of town?

The entrance door to the Gilman House had boarded-over glass. Jack started to pry at the boards but they were nailed fast. A few swift kicks at the doorknob splintered wood and the door swung inward.

"Hello?"

Jack had no idea why he said something aloud. Perhaps the town was just too damn quiet. A glance around the lobby showed a telephone box mounted to the wall. Jack walked across the dirty, faded carpet, glancing at the closed ledger on the reception desk, and a half-loaded rack of room keys behind it.

Cranking the handle desperately, Jack put the receiver to his ear.

"Anyone there? Hello?" he asked into the mouthpiece.

Dead silent, no one was on the other end. The Feds had probably cut the wires and no one from the telephone company was going to bother repairing a phone line in a dead town. Or maybe neglect had set in. Or maybe the phone had been dead for years.

After a few minutes of rhetorical shouting into the mouthpiece, Jack again felt the overwhelming silence of Innsmouth. He was acutely aware of his own fading voice.

Daylight grew stronger, sunlight and shadows were creeping across town. They needed to get out of Innsmouth. They needed to get out before Tommy died, or the authorities came looking into the aftermath of the boat crash. The thought of his wounded brother brought Jack back to reality. He needed to get back, check on Tommy. Then he'd search the town more thoroughly. If he could come up with an automobile. He had heard once, hadn't he - when he was a kid - that Innsmouth folks never got on with horses, so they embraced automobiles more than anyone would think a tiny village would. There had been the bus route, too.

He wondered if the town had a fire engine. He could follow the phone lines from the Gilman House to the firehouse. A small village like Innsmouth would probably only have phones at essential places in town. It was worth a shot.

But, what if they couldn't get out by nightfall? Jack remembered his lessons from the trenches. Be ready for the next fight. Count your ammo. Check your rations. They didn't have rations. Ammo didn't matter. At this point, he might even consider surrendering if they promised medical attention for Tommy. But flashlights would be a boon. He decided on searching the inn for anything they could use, then he'd get back to the church and Tommy.

A quick search behind the lobby desk secured one flashlight. The battery charge was low. The beam was a sickly yellow that barely pierced the gloom of the staircase to the cellar. The dark cellar was the last place Jack wanted to venture but it was the logical place to explore first. The building was old; the rooms would be Spartan at best. The tiny lobby was simply functional. If he hoped to find anything of use, he might find it in the cellar.

There was no medical kit. He found a cabinet of basic hotel needs - a toolbox with miscellaneous, neglected tools. The adjustable wrench too rusty to move; the hammer rusted, too - the head might come off after driving a few more nails; various screws and nails. Anyone who lived near the ocean knew what salt air could do if you didn't upkeep tools. A few larger saws, some dull woodworking knives. Mops and buckets, and some bars of soap and lye. Two more flashlights, both with stronger charges in their batteries and brighter beams.

One of the better flashlights revealed the hole. A gaping maw in the floor, near the corner of the cellar. Against his better judgment, Jack stood at the rim and shined the light beam down. At six feet there was bottom, and then it curved away, down and out of reach of the light. Jack turned to leave, and turned back when he heard the noises.

Scuffing? Shuffling?

He resisted the urge to shout – either in fear or in greeting.

Squatters? Animals?

There were handholds and footholds along the wall of the pit. It was by design, not accident.

Maybe not everyone had left Innsmouth.

If that were the case, why live in tunnels?

What had the Feds found that past February?

Jack forced all those thoughts out of his head. Tommy was wounded. Tommy was his kid brother and Jack needed to help him.

"Hello?" Jack said. His voiced nearly cracked. He had spoken so quietly he wasn't sure he had heard it himself, and yet it sounded too loud in the stillness.

Cursing, Jack made his way down into the dark hole. He remembered the trenches of France. Those were tight but open to the sky. Here the tunnel seemed unnecessarily wide for people, and yet the dark ceiling conveyed great claustrophobic impressions. Jack thought he heard scuffling again. Had he heard a whisper, too?

"I need help," he said into the dark. The walls did not answer.

Jack moved further along. He did not hear any more sounds but his own. Second by excruciating second his confidence slowly rebuilt. He walked with purpose. Until he reached the first branch.

Jack glanced at his watch. Fortunately, it still worked though, like the tools, the soaking it had received would rust it soon. Already he had been absent from his brother's side for too long but curiosity drove him on. He told himself it was necessity. A brisk pace, five-minute reconnoiter on each branch and then if he found no one or nothing he would go back to Tommy.

After fifteen minutes, Jack returned to the first intersection. There had been too many branches. Underground, Innsmouth was a warren. Some of the offshoots followed the roads above, if Jack remembered the town layout and he wasn't too disoriented. Some of the branches didn't. He wondered how long the tunnels had been in place. He wondered how long such a network would take to dig. Maybe they had been bootlegging in Innsmouth. Maybe the Feds had been right. But it felt wrong. Maybe Innsmouth had been smuggling other things. Maybe they'd been smuggling for a very long time. What coastal community hadn't? There had been rumors of Innsmouth gold, after all. Perhaps these tunnels started as pirate hideouts, hundreds of years before.

A sound broke Jack's pondering. A new sound. No longer a scuffling, shuffling. A slithering, squishing sound, like pulling stuck boots from mud. Only with a steady rhythm of movement. Something hissing, too. Or was it sizzling, like lard in a frying pan? Somewhere in the slithering, squishy elements, Jack heard an impossibly high-pitched screech. It was a word, not a scream.

"Tekeli-li!"

Jack ran. Knowing he had the second flashlight in his pocket, Jack spared no moment for the first. He dropped it as soon as his hand reached for the first handhold. The sound grew louder and closer. The closer it came, the more alien it sounded. Jack had heard things most men never had - particularly the screaming of shattered men, mentally and physically. The screech in the tunnels of Innsmouth dug claws into his brain and sanity like those men never had. They had been men, after all. The thing in the tunnel? Jack had no idea and no wish to learn.

Jack spared one glance over his shoulder as he vaulted the rim of the crater. A climbing sprint as good as any over-the-top response he had made when the trench whistles had sounded in France. There might have been the faintest hint of glowing light in the tunnel below. A green, sickly light.

Then it was gone, the sound receding into the dark. Deeper into the underground passages of Innsmouth.

Tommy!

Panic crawled all over Jack. What if Tommy was dead? Jack would be alone. Alone in the world, and worse, alone with that thing crawling under Innsmouth. Jack ran for the church. Whether he used the streets he had used in the earlier darkness, he did not know. He simply kept the steeple in his sights and took a route toward it.

Dread filled the air. Clouds were rolling in. Darkness would come early. Jack panted as he burst through the church entranceway. He physically lurched in reaction when he saw that Tommy no longer occupied the pew. With forlorn hope, he scanned the floor between every pew, in case his brother had wandered or crawled away in delirium.

He found the hole in the back of the church. It had probably been concealed under the floor boards at one time. But the timbers had been shattered, the opening forced. Some fresh dirt and scuff marks indicated recent activity.

Jack was rooted to the spot. He listened for sounds for eternal minutes. He told himself it was caution. Eventually, he admitted to himself it was fear. The admission helped him to take action.

He had to go down into the maw and get his brother the hell out of there.

There were no handholds. Feet first, Jack clumsily slid down the side, freshly disturbed dirt soft under his legs. At the bottom, he wiped his hands against his coat and flicked on the flashlight. The tunnel immediately branched. A large opening and a small. The creature he had seen surely had carved the large orifice. The smaller opening had been hewn out through stone, years ago. Far more human construct. There was no point following the large tunnel. If that thing had Tommy...-

But, maybe Tommy had gotten away, into the smaller tunnel. Dirt raining from above also reminded Jack the fresh tunnel might not be stable. A claustrophobic vision of a wet, damp cave-in made the decision for Jack.

"Tommy?" he asked in a forlorn whisper.

He heard – or imagined he heard – those scuffling, shuffling sounds again. The hair on the nape of his neck stood up but after hearing the other thing, the sounds were welcome. Jack probed ahead with the flashlight. At the furthest edge of the light's beam, something shaped like a man screeched, arms whipped upward to protect the face. Too far away for Jack to see well.

It wasn't Tommy.

It ran. Jack followed.

"Hey! Hey! Wait!"

Jack trotted as fast as he dared along the smooth stone floor. Various side passages passed his field of vision but he pressed on ahead, following the sounds of running feet slapping heavily on the ground.

He paused once. His ears strained to eliminate echoes.

He was sure. Someone – something – had gotten behind him.

He heard those footfalls in front of him and behind him. He tried to tell himself they were echoes but he knew better. The footfalls ahead were growing distant, the footfalls behind consistently increasing in volume and urgency. Jack ran blindly, logic escaping his panicked mind. He wanted to find those ahead, and desperately wanted to escape those from behind. Somewhere in his addled brain he asked himself why not stop and face the pursuers? He had no rational answer. Better to be the hunter, he supposed.

A cry of pain rent the darkness. It was all too human. Jack knew the sound of a wounded man.

"Tommy!"

Jack ran forward, flashlight beam bouncing wildly. The tunnel sloped downward and grew slick with slime and damp. The footfalls from behind increased their pace. The passage emerged into a large chamber. Jack played the light around the space.

The light revealed glistening skin, flecked with silvery piscine scales. Large eyes stared at his intrusion, blinking and screeching as the light reached their exposed pupils. They were standing upright and bipedal. Something human remained in some but they were still warped. These were the survivors, the ones who had already slipped so far from human normalcy that they had probably already been living hidden in the tunnels long before the Feds had razed the waterfront and forcibly evacuated the town above.

Jack nearly went mad at the sight of such corrupted humanity. He spotted his brother's prone body among the horrid denizens. He let out a scream, shoved cold clammy skin and soft bodies aside, tore away a crooked woman who leaned over his brother.

She turned on Jack with a vicious snarl, her skinny arm surprisingly strong and bone-hard smacked him across the face, knocking him down, drawing blood from his mashed lip. His flashlight fell, rolled to a rest, casting its beam against Tommy. Back flat on the stone floor, Jack raised up on his elbows, only to see the deformed woman reach down to Tommy.

She gently patted Tommy's wounded shoulder. Then she made a repeated gurgling noise while she touched his brother. Like a comforting nurse.

In the chaos, and the madness that threatened his mind, Jack processed what he saw. Tommy was bare-chested under his torn coat. The makeshift bandages on Tommy's chest had been changed. They were no longer red with blood. The citizens of Innsmouth had tended Tommy's wound.

Jack's jaw bobbed in silence. He wanted to thank them, he wanted to scream. He didn't believe what he saw and wanted to decry the reality. All the eyes turned to Jack, staring, waiting.

Jack had forgotten his pursuers, and they entered the space now. Jack was unsure if the newest arrivals had any human ancestry in their blood at all. Jagged fish teeth protruded from jutting jaws and swollen lips. Some had small fins where their ears should have been. Others had no such ornamentation obscuring ear canals. Carrying crude fishing spears, they did not even bother with clothing for the most part, though a few wore loincloths.

He saw smaller creatures, hidden between the legs of the larger. Children. Females. By some manner, Jack could tell. Despite the mutations and blasted ancestry, he could tell. They were all females. Females and their offspring.

Jack looked again at the female who doted on his brother.

The eyes of the denizens of the tunnels rounded on him again, expectant.

"You can't think. You can't mean...-"

Jack's head swam. He couldn't tear his gaze away from their eyes. A smell of something indescribably primal but instinctively known cloyed at his nostrils even as he acclimated to the scent.

Their way of life wasn't so far removed from his own, was it? He loved the ocean. He was raised beside it, never wanted to leave its bosom. The waves always crashed in his ears and even when he was so far away, even landlocked in the trenches of France, he had heard the waves whispering for him to come home.

The largest of the females stepped forward and embraced him.

Repulsion fled in the presence of arousal. Jack felt himself harden, penetrate. The clammy flesh entwined his warmth. The earth and the sea, the sand and the water. His senses overwhelmed, he slipped into a trance.

They had a dwindling population but who knew what sort of life-cycles these creatures had? One hundred years might mean nothing to them. Fish fertilized hundreds of eggs at a time, didn't they? One time they might be fortunate, and all the offspring might survive and grow. And flourish.

Cullen saw the future through his rhythmic, thrusting trance. The hordes would swim again. They would sink ships to recreate the damaged reef. They would frolic and splash, and watch the lights of the shore. And on the shore, Innsmouth would rebuild, and grow, and spread their kind among many coastal communities along the coast.

Their time had nearly been cut short but now it approached.

Hundreds?

Jack Cullen would be the father of thousands.

Paul R. McNamee is a lifelong resident of Massachusetts, where he still makes his home with his family. When he's not working his day job or prowling the streets of Arkham, he enjoys reading, writing and book hunting.

Story illustration by **Nikos Alteri**.

Jonas Bell Presents the King in Yellow

by James Pratt

Part 1: Acquisitions Inc.

"So are we gonna fuck this guy up or what?"

Dodger sighed and laid down the battered old copy of *War and Peace* he'd been reading. Trying to read, actually. He'd started it for a fifth time and still hadn't been able to get through the damn thing. Dodger was big on reading. He'd flown through *Little Dorrit* in five-and-a-half days (over a century later and Dickens was still the master), and *The Brothers Karamazov* in an impossible four. But *War and Peace* eluded him.

"What?"

"I said, are we gonna fuck this guy up or what?" It was a question Knuckles asked a lot.

Dodger hated working with Knuckles. No, scratch that. It was Knuckles himself that Dodger couldn't stand. He hated pretty much everything about his sometimes partner; the big man's simplistic outlook on life, those annoying bow ties he wore as some sort of ridiculous affectation, and his gym teacher buzz cut just to name a few. Most of all, he hated Knuckles' stupid nickname. A leg breaker who called himself Knuckles. How original.

Dodger had picked his own nickname ("codename" sounded too stuffy), naming himself after his favorite character from his favorite novel, *Oliver Twist*. All the members of Acquisitions Inc. used aliases, and Dodger was glad he'd been allowed to pick his own. The practice was company policy, and one with which Dodger agreed wholeheartedly.

He glanced at Knuckles who, as usual, looked like an overstuffed sausage. Today's two-sizes-too-small outfit consisted of plaid slacks and an ungodly sports jacket. *Where does this guy shop?* Dodger thought. *1973?* "I don't think that'll be necessary."

"Too bad." Knuckles looked genuinely disappointed. "I got some aggression to work out. Hey, you know what an angry German is?"

"What?"

"A Hessian with aggression." He'd pronounced Hessian as "heh-shun". Knuckles laughed and pounded his meaty fist on the battered end table where Dodger's copy of *War and Peace* lay. "Get it?"

"No." Dodger sighed again. He did that a lot when he had to spend time with Knuckles. "No, I don't get it. Explain it to me."

"Hessian and aggression. It's a pun. You know, because they rhyme."

Dodger rubbed his temples. "That's great, Knuckles. Did you think that one up yourself?"

Knuckles flashed a pearly-white grin. His capped teeth looked way too big for his mouth. "Naw. I saw it on a Bugs Bunny cartoon."

Dodger knew the episode and, as usual, Knuckles got it wrong. It was the one where Yosemite Sam was still fighting the Revolutionary War and, after being bested by his ever-resourceful nemesis, declared, "I'm a Hessian without no aggression." Yosemite Sam was the only thing that had ever elicited a genuine smile from Dodger.

Knuckles rose from the easy chair in which he'd been lounging. "You want something from the fridge?"

"No thanks," Dodger said absently. He'd already eaten and, besides, had no idea what might be stored within the refrigerator in question.

The apartment they currently occupied belonged to neither them nor anyone with whom they were acquainted. The name on the lease was R. William Broadalbin who, by no coincidence, was the gentleman they had come seeking for professional reasons. Three-and-a-half earlier, he had jimmied the lock and he and Knuckles had slipped into his apartment. Mr. Broadalbin was the owner of something someone else wanted to own very, very badly.

That's what Acquisitions Inc. did. Matchmakers of a sort, they placed the desperate with the object of their utmost desire. Satisfaction was 100% guaranteed.

Providing the desperate could afford their fee, of course. *That's how life works*, Dodger thought. *Happiness doesn't come cheap.*

Dodger picked up *War and Peace* and set it down again. He was becoming aggravated and getting a headache. One probably fed into the other. That was another fact of life he'd observed. Most things were a vicious cycle.

Spending time with Knuckles didn't help, but they were stuck here for the duration. They'd gone through the sparsely furnished apartment from top to bottom, but failed to locate the item Acquisitions Inc. had been hired to find. Now they had to do things the hard way, which meant waiting for Mr. Broadalbin to return home and pick his brain regarding the item's current location.

Knuckles preferred doing things the hard way. A team player, he felt that was when he contributed the most. Dodger preferred to slip in and slip out, as quiet and unobtrusive as a shy ghost. He knew Knuckles thought he was a little soft because of the way he preferred to do business, but that was just another example of Knuckles' simplistic outlook. The truth of the matter was that, whereas Knuckles was merely an asshole, Dodger was a borderline sociopath.

A year earlier, Dodger's younger brother had made a tearful, drunken confession. It wasn't something he'd done, but something that had been done to him during their choir boy days. It had only taken Dodger a half-hour to determine that Father Conover was still alive, and another half-hour to discover his current whereabouts. A week later, Dodger paid the priest a visit. The next day, Father Conover was found dangling from a noose. On his desk lay a tear-stained suicide note that served as his final confession. The thing was, Dodger had only been going through the motions. For him, revenge was simply an obligation, like eating or sleeping or screwing.

Knuckles returned and plopped down on a moth-eaten sofa the color of vomit. Virtually all of Mr. Broadalbin's furniture looked like it had been taken from a dump. "The fucking fridge is empty. Who the fuck doesn't keep at least a couple of beers handy?"

Dodger decided to have a little fun. "Why do you say that word so much?"

"What word?"

"Fuck. You say 'fuck' every two seconds."

"So?"

"It's annoying. And vulgar. You sound like a broken record."

"That's just how I express myself," Knuckles replied, sounding a bit defensive. For a guy that broke legs for a living, he could be a little sensitive sometimes.

"If that's how you express yourself then you express yourself in an ignorant fashion."

"What the fuck is that supposed to mean?"

Dodger smiled. He was starting to enjoy himself. "See, there you go. You can't think of anything clever to say so you try to spice things up with a liberal dash of gratuitous 'fucks'."

"Yeah, so?"

"That's self-defeating. By overusing the word, you've lessened its impact. It might have carried some weight once, but now it's just noise."

"Goddamn, man, just get to the fucking point. What are you trying to say?"

"I'm saying that only two kinds of people use the word 'fuck' in any context other than actual fucking. Unimaginative people, by which I mean idiots, and people desperately trying to sound tough. That's what you sound like...a teenager trying to impress his friends by using naughty language."

"Fuck you," Knuckles muttered.

"My point exactly."

Knuckles glared at Dodger, his forehead creased in unaccustomed thought. "You know why I like working with you, Dodger?" he asked after a moment.

"Why's that, Knuckles?" Dodger replied, sounding flippant but actually a little curious.

"Because you don't ask personal questions; you know, try to make small talk or any of that shit. I hate small talk. Fucking despise it." Knuckles pointed toward Dodger. "When you're on the clock, you're all business. I respect that. So that's why I'm wondering if maybe something else is bugging you and you're just taking it out on me."

That caught Dodger off-guard. An Introspective Knuckles? What a strange day it was turning out to be. "You know what? You're right. I…I'm sorry. I suppose I just haven't felt like myself lately. It doesn't help that we've spent the whole afternoon in this crappy little apartment."

"Without a beer in the fridge," Knuckles contributed.

"Without a beer in the fridge, and all for a stupid play."

Knuckles nodded in agreement. "Yeah. Yeah, you're right. This is pretty fu-…pretty freaking aggravating. This is one of those times I wish I knew who we were working for, so I could go find him and kick his ass." That off his chest, he pulled out a comic book and began to read it with a studious intensity.

Clients' identities were supposed to remain anonymous and, while Dodger was a consummate professional in most respects, he also believed he was entitled to anything he could figure out a way to acquire. Curious about why someone would spend so much money to get their hands on an obscure play he'd never even heard of, he did a little research and discovered a few interesting tidbits. The client was none other than Jonas Bell, Broadway's current golden boy. Bell had enjoyed financial success with a string of commercial hits, but critical praise eluded him. From what Dodger could figure, Bell was going for an artsy angle for his next production and nothing said art like pretentious bohemian nonsense. In other words, if you're able to comprehend the plot, establish an emotional rapport with the characters, and temporarily pretend that the events you're watching aren't a staged performance, then it ain't art.

"As for the item they had been sent to acquire, Mr. Broadalbin was in possession of the only known copy of the bizarre play The King in Yellow. The small circle of people familiar with the play only knew of it by its grim reputation in the annals of theater lore. Simply put, the play was said to be cursed. Stories stretching as far back as the late 19th century claimed any attempt to produce The King in Yellow was doomed not just to failure but complete catastrophe. Some reasonably assumed the play itself was nothing more than a legend but that was before an old manuscript had been discovered crumbling away in the dusty depths of the Bibliothèque Nationale de France. The name on the manuscript's title page was Le Roi dans Jaune. English translation: The King in Yellow."

Since then, three attempts had been made to stage a production of *The King in Yellow,* none of which were successful. Each was stalled and ultimately canceled due to a series of unfortunate coincidences and fatal tragedies, including a handful of suicides and three murders among cast and crew. The play eventually became a virtual pariah, a secret no one talked about in the theater community. Every known copy had allegedly been destroyed, burned by the would-be producer of the third attempt to stage it just before he took his own life. Only the original manuscript remained, and its whereabouts was a mystery...at least until Dodger had tracked down Mr. Broadalbin.

A curious tale for a curious play. Dodger was an avowed atheist who believed in a blind, idiot universe ruled exclusively by cause and effect, but even he had to admit the play's history was a bit odd.

Knuckles looked up from his comic book, saw Dodger studying him, and grinned. Dodger sometimes got the impression that Knuckles thought of them as partners. Not in the modern way, but in a more traditional, mythic sense. In Knuckles' mind, they were like rough and ready cowboys in an old John Wayne Western or, better yet, mercenary companions from a sword-and-sorcery novel, making him the Grey Mouser to Knuckles' Fafhrd.

Or George to the big man's Lenny, Dodger thought with a smile.

A key slipped into the lock on the front door. Knuckles smiled. "It's show time."

Yet another cliché. Any sense of camaraderie that Dodger had been feeling for Knuckles evaporated instantly in a cloud of disgust. Moving quietly for such a big guy, Knuckles rose and, with three quick steps, positioned himself so he would be hidden behind the open door. Once Mr. Broadalbin was inside the apartment, he'd be able to block the only exit with a single step. Dodger slipped into the kitchen, where he would wait for Knuckles to speak a greeting to the man they had come to 'interview'. That was the signal for him to suddenly appear, further spooking their target with a rehearsed precision that almost always ensured cooperation with, much to Knuckles' consternation, a minimum of rough stuff.

The door opened and a strange figure entered. Tall and thin, he was dressed in a tattered white overcoat and a wide-brimmed hat pulled low. His features were hidden beneath a thick scarf that covered everything but his eyes, which were a milky cataract-white.

Knuckles gently pushed the door shut. "Howdy," he said with a grin.

The man paused, but didn't turn. He was already looking toward the kitchen when Dodger stepped into view.

Knuckles laid a meaty hand on the man's shoulder. "Hey, buddy, over here." He spun the man around and shoved him against the wall. "Me and my friend here-"

The man's movements were quick and precise. He grabbed Knuckles' face like a bowling ball, inserting his index and middle finger into the eye sockets and thumb in the mouth. Held fast, Knuckles struggled mightily, but in vain. He fumbled ineffectually at the man's face, setting the stranger's hat and scarf askew. The man tossed the hat aside and removed the scarf the rest of the way, revealing a blank, featureless facemask that looked like it had been carved from a single piece of ivory or old bone. Groping for an expression to describe the mask's color, Dodger felt a sense of déjà vu as the curious word "pallid" came to mind.

Blood oozed from Knuckles' eye sockets, staining the sleeve of the man's overcoat and dripping onto the ugly shag carpet that was at least as old as Knuckles' outfit. Heaving, Knuckles made a gurgling sound as a brown, foamy liquid began to dribble from the corners of his mouth. The man slowly lowered his arm, allowing Knuckles to slide to the floor where he laid gagging and whimpering, then turned to Dodger.

Too fascinated to intervene, Dodger had simply stood watching the entire spectacle unfold. As Knuckles slid to the floor, Dodger's hand had slipped beneath his jacket to retrieve the knife he wore everywhere but in the shower (that's what the shower knife was for). Taking a step forward, he froze under the scrutiny of the mask.

"Hello," the man said. From the pronunciation of that single word, Dodger knew that English wasn't the man's native language but he'd mastered it at some point.

"Hello," Dodger replied.

Reaching into the folds of his overcoat, the man produced a scroll case. Like the man's mask, the case appeared to have been carved from a solid piece of bone. Etched into its surface were twisting serpentine shapes.

"I believe this is what you're looking for," the man said, showing the case to Dodger. "Do you know what it is? What it really is?"

Dodger shook his head. He'd seen some strange things in his time, but this…

"Nor should you," the man admitted. "There are some things you just have to see for yourself."

"Who are you?" Dodger asked.

"Many things," the man replied. "That's what the play is, many things. That's the nature of reality, you know, pluralism. Have you ever heard the expression 'It is what it is'?"

Dodger nodded.

"I love that expression. I love binary thinking. It's that very mentality which keeps minds simple and eyes shut.

People who see the world in black and white, who believe a thing is one or the other but never both, only see the tiniest sliver of reality. It makes things easier for the likes of us."

"Us?"

"Those who live in the in-between, who dwell in the places most people choose not to see."

"I...see," Dodger said. The funny thing was, he did see.

"I suppose you're wondering what's going to happen next."

"The thought did occur to me."

"I refused to sell the play to Mr. Bell," the man explained, "because I didn't think he was up to the challenge." A single drop of blood trickled from the tip of his finger as he pointed to Dodger. "Your presence has shown me that I might have misjudged him. It takes mettle for a man of his background to consort with the likes of you. No offense."

Dodger shrugged. "None taken."

"Now that I've changed my mind, he may have it with my blessing."

The man extended the case to Dodger. After a moment, Dodger slid the knife back into its sheath, reached toward the case, and took it. Retaining his grip, the man locked eyes with Dodger for a moment then released the case.

"Why do you wear that mask?" Dodger asked.

"I'm not wearing a mask."

"No?"

"No," the man replied. "There are no masks, only faces within faces."

"All that stuff about the play…The curse…"

"There's no such thing as curses." The man stepped aside and gestured toward the door. "Tell Mr. Bell that I am looking forward to his production and that I will be there, sitting in the front row, on opening night."

A few hours later, Dodger sat in his small, modestly furnished apartment. The TV was off, as usual, and the scroll case lay unopened on the table before him. He felt foolish. He'd never welched on a job before, and he hadn't seen anything in the past couple of hours that couldn't be reasonably explained. Maybe the man, Mr. Broadalbin, was a trained martial artist, or was just plain lucky when he got the drop on Knuckles.

Dodger had no idea why he was even entertaining thoughts of chucking the manuscript. He was unaccustomed to being disgusted with himself, or to feeling much of anything. The whole thing was simply ridiculous. But the stuff Broadalbin had said…Dodger had no idea what the man had been trying to tell him. Maybe he wasn't supposed to get it. Maybe Broadalbin was just having some fun with him.

A cursed play that caused insanity…it was ridiculous. Still, there had been three recorded attempts to stage the play and each had been thwarted by death and madness. Broadalbin had said Jonas Bell was the right man for the job. So what would happen if someone actually managed to stage the play?

And what was Broadalbin hiding behind that mask? Dodger vaguely recalled coming across something called the 'Pallid Mask' during his research of the play, which would explain why the word 'pallid' had come to mind. In the play, the mask is worn by a character known as the 'Phantom of Truth' and where the Phantom of Truth appears, the titular King in Yellow soon follows.

Dodger took a deep breath and sighed. He had no experience with ethical dilemmas, if that's what was happening. Then an idea struck him. Maybe there was a way to find out. Dodger picked up the scroll case, unscrewed the lid, and carefully removed the manuscript.

Dodger had momentarily forgotten that the manuscript was in French but that didn't matter. He'd taught himself to read the language so he could read French novels in their native tongue. But it wasn't too late to turn back. He could simply replace the manuscript in its case, turn it over to his employer, and wait for his next assignment.

But now he was curious. He *had* to know. Taking another deep breath, he unfurled the manuscript and started to read.

Part 2: Opening Night

Jonas Bell took a sip from the silver flask, savoring the sweet, sweet burn as it trickled down his throat. The flask had been a gift from the late, great Elias Hughes. The one-time toast of Broadway, Hughes had served as Jonas's mentor, surrogate father-figure, and only homosexual experience in that order. It was a bittersweet memento of the man who had taught him so much, and from whose shadow he feared he would never escape. After tonight, he hoped, no one would bother mentioning them in the same sentence again. After tonight, Jonas would be in a class all by himself.

Desperate times calling for desperate measures, Jonas had paid a sizeable sum (over half his savings, in fact) for the "by any means necessary" acquisition of the parchment manuscript which represented his possible salvation. Tucked away in a battered old lockbox in Jonas's desk was the only known copy of the spectacularly obscure play *The King in Yellow*. Its existence was known only to a select few, and most of them believed it was the theatrical equivalent of an old wives' tale. Jonas considered all this and smiled. They'd know the truth soon enough.

Jonas hadn't felt this nervous since his first starring role in elementary school. Opening night jitters, the hacks called it. His little heart had pounded like a jackhammer as he stood in the wings, waiting for his cue to set foot on stage where he would portray Bottom in a watered-down 6th grade production of *A Midsummer Night's Dream*. The instant his mouth opened to speak Bottom's first line, he'd been transported to a magical forest where a fortuitous mingling of accident and design taught lessons of the heart to fairies and mortals alike.

Jonas drained the flask dry and returned it to its hiding place. His father had called it 'liquid courage', and it was something Jonas thought he'd never need again. Fresh out of college, his star had begun a Faustian rise; for Jonas, there had been nowhere to go but up. He had fame, success, money in the bank. He was the rarest creature in the world, a successful Broadway director, and it should have been enough.

Love wasn't the only thing money couldn't buy, and even love could be rented by the hour. Respect was what Jonas craved. It was ironic, really. He and his theater friends used to joke about critics, how they were frustrated wanna-be artists who exorcised their inner demons by tearing down the creations of others. Who would have thought the day would come when Jonas would give his left, and only remaining, testicle for a positive review?

And oh, how the critics loved to hate him...

"Jonas Bell's heavy-handed direction was enough to sink even The Unsinkable Molly Brown," that smug, pimply-faced fat-ass Arthur Seles had written in the Post.

"Bell's production of You Oughta Be in Pictures *was so saccharine, one would be fortunate not to acquire type-2 diabetes while viewing it,"* was the clever summation of one Milton Quinn, who had probably been busy fondling the genitals of a male prostitute half his age while writing it.

God, how he hated critics. Talentless bastards, every one. What was it Elias used to say? "Familiarity breeds contempt, success more so". Jonas had even come up with one of his own: Those who can't do, teach and those who can't teach become critics. They attacked him with a vengeance, almost as if it were personal. But he was the real thing. He'd show them. Jonas had already proven he could make money. Now he'd show them he could make art.

Of course, a real artist was willing to pay for his art and Jonas had done just that. It had cost him a pretty penny, and required consorting with the sort of people he'd once thought only existed in gangster movies, but he'd gotten it. Locked away in his desk was the only known copy of *The King in Yellow,* perhaps the most obscure and infamous play in existence. Sure, he'd heard the rumors, but that just added to the mystique. Tonight, Jonas Bell would make-

"Mr. Bell?"

Jonas spun, nearly falling out of his seat. Standing in the doorway was a tall man, lean and broad-shouldered, with dark circles under his eyes and a week's growth of beard. He wore a shabby overcoat, under which Jonas glimpsed a weird uniform with a 1950s-era sci-fi retro-futuristic vibe.

Jonas had been jumpy since the Lisbon incident, when he'd experienced first-hand the dark side of celebrity. Still, he couldn't help but feel a little bit macho whenever he saw his own reflection and noted the souvenir scar on his left cheek. "Um, yes, I'm Jonas Bell. Can I help you?"

The man practically collapsed into a chair. "At last. My name is Thale."

"Thale?" The name seemed familiar. *Oh, right,* Jonas thought. "Like in the play?"

"What? Oh, right, of course." The man flashed an unsettling grin. "Just like in the play."

Great, Jonas thought. *Another method actor.* "Are you here to try out for the part of Thale? You do realize that since tonight is opening night, it's probably safe to assume the part's been taken."

Still smiling, the man shook his head. "No, I am not here for that. That would be like you trying out for the part of Jonas Bell. Of course, it could be argued..." The man's voice trailed off and his eyes became vacant.

"Um...Mr. Thale? You okay?"

Thale blinked, refocused on Jonas, and waved a dismissive hand. "Never mind. That is a conversation for another day. Metaphysical causality was never my strong point."

"Ah. Um...Look, I don't mean to be rude, but I really have a lot of last minute things to take care of. That's what

I get for being a procrastinator, right?" Jonas flashed his most charming grin, but Thale simply stared at him. "Okay, what is it exactly I can do for you?"

Thale's grim smile vanished. "The play. You must not put it on. It is not your fault. You do not realize what you are doing, but you have to stop."

"Stop the…why would I want to do that? Do you have any idea how much trouble I've gone through to stage this thing? Did you know that there was just one manuscript of the original play in existence? You wouldn't believe what I had to go through to get my hands on it."

"To earn it?" the man asked.

"What?" Jonas thought for a moment. "Yeah. Yeah, that's right. I earned it, and I earned the right to put this thing on even if it kills me."

Thale slowly leaned forward. "That would be the least of your worries."

Jonas's eyes narrowed. "What's that supposed to mean?"

"If you put this play on, there will be blood on your hands, Mr. Bell."

"What are you…?" Jonas's right hand nonchalantly crept toward the upper-right desk drawer where he kept the gun he'd carried since Lisbon. "Are you threatening me, Mr. Thale?"

"No." Thale ran his right hand through a greasy tangle of shoulder-length hair. "Look, I have come a long way. My brother Uoht and I set out what seemed like a million years ago. He is…he is dead now. The *hounds* got him."

Uoht was, in fact, Thale's brother in the play. So the Thale sitting in his office had done his homework. "Set out from where?"

"From Yhtill. Our mother sent us at the request of the priest Noatalba. Being the most sensitive, he was the first to notice it. It did not take long for the rest of us to notice, though. You see, whenever someone reads the play, we know. Our world changes around us as a new set of eyes interpret the words to suit themselves, even as the play begins to change the reader's world around them."

Not a method actor, Jonas thought. *Just a fruitcake. Then again, what's the difference?* "You know these people and places are works of fiction, right?"

Thale smiled bitterly. "We are all works of fiction, Mr. Bell. Is not life just a story being written by some greater author, be it the gods, or blind destiny, or whatever you want to call it? Self-determination is an illusion."

"Look, I'd love to have a philosophical discussion with you, but this really isn't a good...Wait a minute. Is this about that stupid curse?" Jonas knew all about the stories of murders and suicides associated with *The King in Yellow.* The rumors claimed that no one had ever been able to stage a full performance of the play, and no one ever would. That, of course, was part of its appeal. "If this is a joke, I really don't-"

"No." Thale's expression darkened. "No joke."

"Then you're really here about the curse?"

"The problem isn't a curse. It's not even really a play."

"No? Then what is it?"

"Many things. It's a historical record...a prison...a..." Thale thought for a moment. "An incantation."

"What, like a spell?"

Thale nodded.

"And what happens when the spell is cast."

"*Un*cast, you mean. Performing the play uncasts the spell, for it has already been cast. Millennia ago...or perhaps millennia hence. I'm not sure how it works."

"Those binding spells can be tricky," Jonas observed with a straight face.

"And were you to succeed," Thale continued, "then *he* who is the hideous dream of the Unspeakable One will be loosed. *He* will come to your world as he did to mine, when *he* descended from Aldebaran in the Hyades to throw down my ancestor, the first Aldones, and lay claim to fabled Carcosa."

"Oh. Well why didn't you say so in the first place? That sounds a lot more reasonable than a curse." Jonas flashed a good natured grin, but saw that Thale wasn't biting. "Do you really think something bad's going to happen if the play is staged?"

Thale leaned back. "*Has* anything bad happened?"

"No. I mean, there's always going to be some sort of..." Jonas sighed. "Okay, okay, a stagehand was killed by a falling light. That was the first fatality during any of my productions, but accidents happen all the time. I'm sure most of them don't involve a curse. I'm sorry, an incantation."

Thale nodded. "Anything else?"

I don't need this, Jonas thought. "There's been some...trouble with the crew. A lot of fights. And..."

"And?"

Jonas sighed. "One of our understudies disappeared. At first we thought she'd just dropped out of the production but it turned out nobody had heard from her in days."

"Is that it?"

"Well...there was a triple murder a few days ago in the alley outside, but this is New York. People get murdered here all the time."

"Anything else?"

"I'm sure it's just a coincidence, but some-"

"Enough." Thale rubbed his eyes. "I am tired, and this conversation is pointless. Listen to me. I have traveled far, farther than you could imagine. It was one of your rehearsals that let us come through."

"Us?"

"My brother and I. I thought I already mentioned him. We came here to stop it from...happening again. They knew the moment we came through. We made it to the outskirts of this city before the Brotherhood caught up with us..." Thale's voice trailed off again.

"Brotherhood?"

"The Brotherhood of the Yellow Sign."

"Right," Jonas said. "The Yellow Sign, like in the play. The symbol of the King in Yellow."

Thale nodded. "They were waiting for us. Somehow they knew. The Brotherhood's reach spans realities, even to far Tindalos in the void. It was the Tindalos *hounds* that got Uoht. They came right out of the walls. All they need to materialize is an angle, and the odd architecture here supplies them in abundance. Frankly, it amazes me that all these flat edges do not drive you insane."

That's an ironic thing to say, Jonas thought. *Then again, crazy people never believe they're crazy.* "What do you mean 'my world'? Where do you come from, exactly?"

Thale pointed in the direction of the manuscript, which was tucked away in a lockbox in the bottom left desk drawer.

"You're saying you literally come from the play?"

Thale shook his head. "The play is a touchstone, for lack of a better word. Not so much between worlds as between possibilities." He shrugged. "It is hard to explain."

"Try," Jonas said, not sure whether he was curious or stalling for time.

"The play is mostly...what's the word? Metaphor, I think." Thale nodded. "Yes, it is mostly a metaphor. But the story it tells is real, or maybe it is the telling that makes it real. I am not a meta-physicist. I do not know how it works but, like I said, it was your rehearsals that allowed Uoht and me to come through." He was silent for a moment, eyebrows knotted. "Maybe that is how it works. It *makes* things real by changing the world to match the story, like a...a virus infecting reality."

"Maybe it's the ultimate example of reality imitating art," Jonas said. "But if that's the case and the world remains mostly unchanged, then how do you fit into all this? Where do you really come from?"

"Maybe..." Thale scratched his stubbly chin. "Maybe I am just some transient who was appropriated for this role and all my memories...of my beloved mother and hated father, of my beautiful sister Camillia, of the glorious kingdom of Yhtill and its endless feud with the hated Alar, of the horrors lurking within the cloudy depths of the Lake of Hali, even of the cursed Carcosa itself...are just fabrications."

"If it's possible that you didn't come from some other world, isn't it also possible that you somehow came into contact with a translation of the play? I've heard there are some copies floating around out there. Now, I'm not a psychiatrist but it's obvious you're in some sort of...distress. Maybe something happened to you and you used the vivid imagery of the play to create a new reality of your own." Jonas paused for a moment and looked at Thale, who was watching him intently. "Hey, stranger things have happened. Now, let's take it a step further. Maybe your desire to stop the play, and thereby thwart this reality you've created, is really your subconscious trying to guide you back to the real world."

Thale was silent for a moment. "Would that I could believe that, but the memories are too real. I can remember the smell, the texture of things. I can remember the sound of Camilla's voice, the warmth of her touch and deviousness of her smile. Even now, I recall the look of betrayal on my father's face as he was banished from Yhtill by his own wife, my mother Cassilda. She was not content to be a mere consort, you see." He sighed and shook his head. "It does not matter. Regardless of which reality is the real one...yours, mine, both, neither...there are forces at work here which must be acknowledged and...dealt with."

Jonas swallowed. "Look, I think maybe you need to talk to someone who's better equipped to help you." He started to reach toward his desk phone, which sat on the corner above the drawer where his pistol lay.

Thale shoved him back in his seat. "Fool! You have not heard one word I've said! Do you not realize I am trying to save you? I am trying to keep it from happening here!"

"Keep what from happening here? What do you think is going to happen? It's just a play. The worst thing that can happen is a bad review! I can handle that. I'm used to those."

Thale slammed his fist on the desk. "It's already started! Can you not see that? Ill luck and violence are only the beginning. Simply reading it is enough to draw *his* attention, thus the misfortune. Where *his* gaze falls, there can be naught but misery and woe. If you were able to actually perform it from start to finish, then...then *he* would come through and it would be the end of everything."

"Who would come through?"

"The King in Yellow! Who do you think?" Thale took a deep breath. "Those deaths you mentioned. That is how it starts...tragedies that could be ascribed to coincidence. Has anything else happened-", he motioned toward the window, "-out there?"

"Well...there are the Cannibal Killings."

"Cannibal Killings?"

"There's a serial killer out there who partially eats the bodies of his victims."

"When did these killings start?"

"About the same time we...It's just the work of a serial killer. A sick person. You can't prove there's any sort of connection between the play and that. That's ridiculous."

"It was no sick person. It was the dead. The play makes them restless, and the dead always wake up hungry."

"You mean zombies? That's insane." Jonas winced at his own choice of words. "Look, I'm sorry, but I'm going to have to ask you to leave. I have a lot of work to do. So unless there's anything else I can do for you..."

Jonas' voice trailed off as Thale reached into his overcoat and produced a long knife.

"I am sorry, too, Mr. Bell," Thale said. "I have not done a very good job of explaining the gravity of the situation. Even though I have seen these things with my own eyes and know for a fact everything I have said is true, I can understand how strange it all must sound. Words were never my strong point. Uoht was always better at that sort of thing. He was the scholar, like father." He stared at the knife, watching the light play on its blade. "Me, I hated books. The only thing I enjoyed studying was swordplay." Thale looked at Jonas. "There is only one way to stop the play then. If there was any other way..."

Thale took a step toward Jonas, who was already in motion. He pulled the gun from his desk drawer, pointed it at Thale, and pulled the trigger. The gun produced a muted click. Thale and Jonas stared at each other, as if comically frozen by the awkwardness of the situation. "Goddamit!" Jonas hissed, clicking the safety off. By the time he pulled the trigger again, Thale loomed over him, knife upraised. Jonas couldn't help but notice how the sight and sound of a real gun discharging was so much less dramatic than on television or in the movies, where the boom of a discharged weapon held all the authority of the voice of God himself.

Thale stumbled backwards, a look of confusion on his face. "But..."

Jonas pulled the trigger again. Thale jerked and stumbled backward, crashing through the window he'd looked through moments earlier and tumbling out of sight.

Slack-jawed, Jonas stared at the window. He slowly rose, approached it, and looked out. Below lay the dirty alley just as it had been when he'd arrived that morning, albeit with the addition of a sprinkling of shattered glass.

"Jonas?" Erin, his assistant and part-time lover, was standing in the doorway and staring at the smoking pistol in his hand.

"I hit him," Jonas stammered. "Right in the chest. I know I did. I saw the blood..."

"Hit who?"

"The man. The man in the ragged coat."

"What man?"

"The...the man. Thale. He called himself Thale, like in the play. Surely you saw him come in. It's not like he didn't stand out. I mean..."

Erin shrugged. "I didn't see anybody come in."

"He was here. I swear to God he was...here." Jonas gently laid the gun on his desk. "I...uh...I don't know what's happening here." He stumbled backwards, and nearly fell over his desk.

Erin rushed over and guided Jonas into his chair. "Sit down. I'll get you something to drink. You've been under a lot of pressure lately. I know how much this play means to you. It's okay. Even the great Jonas Bell is human. You're allowed to get stressed out once and awhile." She picked up the pistol and held it gingerly. "I'll just put this in a safe place."

After she was gone, Jonas locked the door to his office, retrieved the lockbox that held the manuscript, and unrolled it across his desk. The strange characters seemed to crawl over the parchment, as restless and predatory as a hungry viper. Jonas never told anyone he'd gone through seven translators to get the full script in English, or what happened to said translators. He recalled the haunted look on the face of the small, sharp-featured man who'd delivered it to him. He thought of the face he now saw looking back at him whenever he dared glance into a mirror. It was his face, but aged ten years. It was the face waiting for him on the far side of some great tragedy looming in his future. Shaking the cobwebs from his head, Jonas returned the manuscript to its proper place.

Maybe Thale, whomever he was, had been right after all. Maybe the play really was more than just a play. Maybe it was a portal to some unimaginable place, or a virus that infected reality itself. Maybe watching it guaranteed the audience a quick descent to madness or worse. And maybe, just maybe, that audience would include Arthur Seles and Martin Quinn.

"Showtime," Jonas said, and bit back a laugh. He was pretty sure if he did start laughing, he wouldn't be able to stop.

Part 3: The Show Must Go On

-and the corpses were walking, and there was a terrible awareness in their eyes. These weren't shambling, mindless horrors; they remembered what they had been and knew what they had become. The only horror about them was the horror in the expressions they wore, the only fear was the fear of what they now knew and the hideous secrets they might reveal. The dead mingled freely with the living, for in this place, there was little difference between the two. In this place, life and death were merely roles to be played as required.

The scene shifted, granting a bird's-eye view of a vast lake rushing by below. On the eastern shore was Alar, a city of onyx draped in perpetual gloom. It sprawled across the land like a bloated spider in whose glittering eyes were ever reflected the light of unknown stars. On the western shore sat Yhtill; a metropolis of high-reaching towers adorned in precious stones, it was a sacred city consecrated to infant gods no older than Yhtill itself. Ancient enemies they were, united only in their common fear of the thing which lay dead and dreaming beneath the still, black waters of the accursed Lake of Hali. Indeed, they were as one in their terror of the unspeakable thing whose name no one dared pronounce.

Something stirred within Hali's cloudy depths, and the world trembled. The scene lost focus, wavering as if seen through a blue-white cascade of rushing water. It then resolved itself into a barren plain where strange figures, man-shaped but hairy and tusked, emerged from mud huts to brandish stone-headed axes as they howled at the sky. The plain soon gave way to frozen tundra where white-furred bear-like monstrosities, six-legged and fiery-eyed, paused in their grisly feast to momentarily raise their crimson snouts and regard the heavens. The scene accelerated, flying by ever faster, and the landscape was reduced to a featureless gray monotony. Perspective vanished, greedily gobbled up in the dizzying progression until gray dissolved to black.

An age passed in the space of a heartbeat, and perspective was restored. Black faded to gray as titan mountains reared up on the horizon, their collective shadow a shroud of despair cast upon the cold, dead earth. Up the mountainside, the scene flew past icy peaks infested with quivering, boneless things that mewled 'Tekeli-li! Tekeli-li!' as they quivered and flopped beneath the dying light of a blood-red sun.

And there, on the far side of the greatest peak, lay the silent valley where one world ended and another began.

"It is the Womb of Mother Singularity," a phantom voice insisted.

"The Eye of Azathoth," another voice whispered.

"It is the threshold," yet a third voice proclaimed. "The place where worlds are born in the dreams of gods, and gods are born in the dreams of men."

In the heart of the valley the scene progressed, soaring over the empty vastness of a great gulf where survivals from forgotten ages hid themselves away from the eyes of the world. From out of the dreary gloom a sad voice sang...

"Held fast within the grip of night

There were no stars within our sight,

Save only the pale and fitful light

Of the jewel which hangs o'er lost Carcosa."

There, on the far side of the gulf and framed in the ghost-light of the red star Aldebaran in the Hyades, it lay. It was the city, the first true city, and nothing within it drew breath. There, at last, lay Carcosa.

Somewhere within its dusty depths, dream knowledge instructed, the bones of its builder lay. Carcosa was the crowning achievement of Aldones, the first true king, and meant to be the jewel of his empire. But Aldones dreamed too high and reached too far. With *the rising of Aldebaran, magnificent Carcosa fell under the scrutiny of one who is the waking dream of the unspeakable dweller in the Lake of Hali. And so, with the rising of Aldebaran in the Hyades, Aldones' masterpiece became his tomb.*

Beneath an archway of carved bone, an ivory mask floated above robes of funereal white that hung spectral in the air. An empty sleeve beckoned, and the vision was gone. Beyond the archway, the scene became a mad dash through labyrinthine, skull-cobbled streets, past protean statuary which marked the progress of the star Aldebaran above, straight to the windowless tower at the heart of Carcosa. Now the scene paused, a dream afraid to proceed, before the tower's single portal above which was inscribed the swirling rune of the Yellow Sign. But proceed it did, through the portal, down stone stairs that wound deep into the earth, to a vast chamber in which nothing had stirred for millennia. Now the scene wavered, a dream in terror of itself, but it was too late to look away, too late to turn back.

Perspective panned upward, slow and inevitable, to behold the lord of Carcosa. A hooded apparition draped in the chains of a penitent ghost and swathed in an archaic ochre shroud, it hovered high in the air though its ragged hem hung low enough to touch the ancient throne upon which the bones of the first Aldones sat. The apparition was motionless, not so much an inanimate statue as the phantom centerpiece of a single moment severed from the flow of time. The folds of its shroud were frozen mid-flutter, as if whipped by a furious wind. The apparition's raised right sleeve pointed southward toward the Lake of Hali because that was the cradle of the dreamer in whose dream the world was born. Pinpoints of feeble light flickered at the end of the sleeve, the Hyades in miniature, at the heart of which glowed the red star like a single fiery eye.

Nothing had disturbed the silence, nor stirred the corpse-dust within the chamber since the fall of the first Aldones. Then, without warning, the chains fell away and the cowled head slowly began to turn. The King in Yellow was-

Jonas Bell jerked awake. "Christ," he rasped, "the chains were my idea." He tried to swallow, but his throat was parched. He tried to sit up, but his body was too weak. Worst of all was the itch, like ants crawling over most of his body.

Jonas took stock of his surroundings. He lay beneath starched sheets on a stiff mattress in a high bed with metal railings. The bed sat in the center of a generically furnished room that smelled of antiseptics. A television bolted to the wall was silent. A thin tube ran from an IV drip to his left arm.

"Welcome back to the land of the living."

The lights were off and the shades hung low so Jonas squinted into the gloom. A figure stood in the corner, a gray smudge hidden in shadow. "Who are you?"

The man stepped into the light. Tall and narrow, he wore a long overcoat, a scarf pulled up over most of his face, and a wide-brimmed hat, all of which were an ivory shade of white. "We have never been introduced, but you should think of me as a friend. Better yet, a patron."

"Water," Jonas pleaded.

The man quickly obliged, filling up a nearby cup, inserting a straw, and holding the cup to Jonas' mouth while he greedily sipped.

"Where am I?" Jonas asked after he'd drunk the cup dry. "Is this a hospital?"

The man nodded.

"How did I get here?"

"You were brought here by an ambulance. I dragged you out of the theater myself."

"The theater?"

"Oh yes. It was an opening night no one will forget."

Memories came rushing back. "Oh. Oh, God."

"Such a performance." The man clapped his hands softly. "Bravo, Mr. Bell. Well done."

Jonas stared hard at the man. "I remember you. You were there, sitting right in the front row. You stood out because you were dressed head to toe in white. Even though I couldn't see your..." The man's most distinguishing feature that night had been a white featureless mask, a pale buoy in a sea of faces. "Who did you say you were?"

"Merely an admirer of your work, and yes, I was there...front row, center as promised. I wouldn't have missed it for the world."

"I...I remember a little bit. The screaming, the...the fire." Jonas swallowed as his head sank back into the pillow. "What happened?"

"It was glorious," the man said. "Under your able direction, the players made it halfway through the second act. That's farther than I got. Farther than anyone has ever gotten."

"How many died?"

The man shrugged. "Does it matter?"

"Does it matter? What kind of..." Jonas couldn't concentrate. The itching was driving him mad. "Thale was right. He was right about everything." He raised his hands to scratch his face and paused, noticing for the first time they were swathed in bandages.

"You spoke to Thale?" The man considered that for a moment. "I am surprised he was the one that made it. Perhaps I did not give the idiot enough credit. I always thought Uoht was the bigger threat. Neither could hold a candle to their mother though."

Jonas thought of the conversation he'd had with the man who'd introduced himself as Thale, one of the princes from *The King in Yellow*, only hours before the first and last performance. "Was he the real Thale? From the play?"

The man shrugged. "Real enough. Depends on your definition of reality, I suppose. Do you know where he is, by any chance? I would love to see him again. It would be like a...family reunion."

"I...shot him. He'd dead."

"Ah." The man sighed. "Just as well."

"Oh, God," Jonas moaned. "I really shot him. I'd almost convinced myself the whole thing was just my imagination, but he was real and I shot him. He tried to warn me and, deep down, I knew he was right. I knew what was going to happen. The blood of all those people is on my hands."

The man patted Jonas' shoulder. "Well, if it is any consolation, you did not exactly kill Thale. He passed from the realm of flesh and blood a long time ago. Traded it for immortality of a sort. Thale is not so much a man as an idea, a concept. You can do all sorts of things with a concept...modify it, appropriate it, but you cannot kill it." He walked over to a nearby chair and sat down. "Now the audience, on the other hand, they were most certainly flesh and blood."

"Oh, God," Jonas repeated.

The man held up a gloved hand. "Oh, it's not as bad as all that. There were a few survivors. You have done them a favor, changed them forever. You lifted the veil from their eyes, if only for a moment, to give them a glimpse of the horrors beneath. They are prophets now, spreading the word even as we speak."

Jonas closed his eyes. He thought he should be crying, but felt no tears. "I can still hear the screams."

"Screams?" The man shook his head. "Those were the voices of the faithful raised in worship, singing songs of praise. They were not your audience. They were his congregation."

"Who?" Jonas tried to recall what Thale had said about the bad thing that would happen if the play were performed from start to finish. Something about the titular King in Yellow himself...

"So close," the man said wistfully. "*His* eyes were upon us. I could feel *him* watching. If only you had finished, he would have come through. I just know it." The man sighed. "So close..."

"Still," he continued, "under your able direction, your humble little company made it farther than anyone else ever has before. Even farther than I did, and I know the story intimately. I know now that I made the right choice in you."

"What are you saying? What would have happened if we'd gotten all the way through?"

The man's head cocked to one side. "You have read the play, haven't you?

"Of course I have. I just...I can't quite remember..."

"You already know how it ends."

"The King in Yellow appears. That's what Thale said would..." Jonas shook his head. "No, this is ridiculous. It's just a play. I've seen nothing that...well, I've seen plenty, but nothing that can't be explained rationally."

"Really. And what would be the rational explanation for what happened halfway through the second act?"

"I...I don't remember what happened."

"Come now, Mr. Bell. You do not remember what really started the riot? It will be blamed on the fire, but the fact of the matter is that the mad dash for the exits was already well under way before the fire began. They got a peek of what was waiting on the other side. One glimpse was all it took." The man chuckled softly. "Do you know how people are like cattle, Mr. Bell? When push comes to shove, they will commit criminally desperate acts in the name of self-preservation which, ironically, only serves to create one big obstruction blocking any means of egress. You want to watch people die in a stampede? Yell 'fire'. The fire itself is optional. Just yell the word, and human nature will take care of the rest."

Jonas again reached for his face to scratch the incessant itching only to discover it was covered with bandages. "Why are there bandages on my face?"

"You really do not remember what happened?" The man sighed and shook his head. "This is rather awkward. Still, better you should learn from me than some dispassionate sawbones." The man reached into his overcoat, produced a small mirror, and held it up to Jonas's face. "Behold."

"Oh….Oh my God." Jonas squeezed his eyes shut, the brief glimpse of the reflection seared into his mind. The bandages were wound thick and tight, but his eyes, mouth, and the areas around them were exposed, revealing not so much flesh as charred meat covered in waxy rivulets of half-melted skin.

The man hastily withdrew the mirror. "Regrettable, yes, but think of it as a temporary inconvenience." He removed his hat, revealing wisps of white hair that clung to flesh the color and consistency of cracked leather and stretched taut over an oddly elongated skull. "Better yet, a step in your evolution."

The scene seemed terribly familiar, the inevitable conclusion to a chain of events stretching farther back than Jonas could imagine. "What are you doing?" he asked, not wanting an answer.

The man slid the scarf free, but his features remained hidden beneath a smooth ivory mask. "See, I have brought you a new face."

"A mask?" Jonas tried, and failed, to smile. "Okay, okay, I get it now. First Thale shows up, now it's the Pallid Mask. It's what the Phantom of Truth wore, the King in Yellow's herald in the play. So that's who you're supposed to be."

"I always preferred the term 'advocate'. And I wear no mask." He pointed to Jonas's ruined features. "Beneath those bandages is the mask you have worn your entire life. It is time to show the world your face." He stroked the ivory mask. "Your real face.

"My real face?" Jonas's stomach was doing somersaults, the way it always did when he felt a sense of anticipation, dread, or a combination of the two. "I don't understand."

The man gave his shoulder a squeeze. "Thanks to your prodigious talent, you have earned a great honor. On a personal note, I can assure you I could not be more grateful. I am not getting any younger, you know."

"You...you want me to wear the mask?"

"There is a little more to it than that. It comes with certain...responsibilities."

Jonas's eyes narrowed. "Who are you really?"

"Whomever the scene calls for. The last sorcerer of the line of Aldones. The once and future king of glorious Yhtill. A betrayer who was betrayed by those he loved the most." The man shrugged. "I am afraid the role requires a bit of improvisation. Intrigue is a young man's game."

Jonas struggled to sit up. Whatever was about to happen was only moments away. "And what is the play?"

"Again, whatever is called for. An odd bit of theater to some, the holy writ of an ancient god to others. Those of an occult bent might describe it as an incantation in two acts, a spell of binding which, once undone, will grant an entity of vast and terrible power ingress into the magician's reality. And no mere *cacodaemon* at that. We are talking end of the world stuff here."

"Christ, can't you just give me a straight answer?"

"Have you not been listening? There are no straight answers! But..." The man's voice dropped to a theatrical whisper, "I will tell you my personal favorite. Imagine that scene over a million years ago, the landscape bathed in the red light of Aldebaran as the King in Yellow descended upon Carcosa where he would rule for millennia. Ages hence, a descendent of the first Aldones and who also bears his ancestor's name, comes seeking the aid of Carcosa. He has been betrayed by those he loves most and desires retribution. Standing before a dusty throne, he invokes the Covenant of the Yellow Sign which binds the line of Aldones to Carcosa."

"I don't–"

"Bear with me. This Aldones, the last living sorcerer of that sacred line, is given an item of power in the form of the Pallid Mask. It is a potent gesture, but also a sham. The Pallid Mask cares only for the will of its one true master, and he who wears the mask is but a puppet of Carcosa. Seeing that he has once more been betrayed, this Aldones weaves one last enchantment. He binds Carcosa to a realm farther removed from the land of the living than the realm of death itself...the realm of legend. And so the King in Yellow is removed from the world, and chained in a prison of words."

"But it doesn't end there," the man continued. "Aldones overreaches. By the time he realizes what he has done, it is already too late. He has bound his entire world within the play and, having used up most of his strength in the binding, cannot undo what he has done. And so he begins searching for the one who does have the strength. It is a long journey that goes on to this very day."

The man wrenched the Pallid Mask from his face with some effort. Jonas caught a glimpse of a ruined face into whose withered cheeks color was already starting to return. "Just think, you might be there when the play is finally performed from start to finish."

Jonas shook his head. "This is...I don't..."

The man, the last sorcerer of the line of Aldones or whomever he was, raised the mask and pressed it toward Jonas' face. "The mask wants its master to be free. That is the only way you will ever be rid of it. I truly hope you succeed, for your sake as well as mine. Imagine the sights you will see, the wonders you will behold. As for me, I just want to go home."

Jonas tried to push the mask away, but the man's strength was irresistible. "No. I don't want it. I don't want it."

The mask drew closer and closer until it occupied Jonas's entire field of vision-

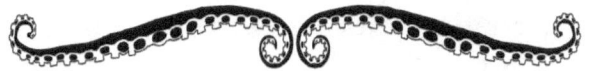

The door to the room opened and a small man with thin, predatory features peered in. "Mr. Bell?" Nothing stirred within the room. The only sign of life was an empty hospital gown that lay beneath crumpled sheets on the bed.

"Damn," Dodger hissed.

It had taken him a few days to decide to act. He was a rational man but the things that had happened when he'd tried to read the play…haunted house stuff culminating in the dream of a strange city in a strange land. Dodger had been tempted to destroy it. In the end, he'd decided his professional reputation was at stake. A man's reputation was the only thing he really owned, as his father used to say. Then the opening night incident had gone and validated his first impulse, and Dodger had been forced to admit he'd screwed up big time.

What was done was done. Now all Dodger could do was try to keep things from going any farther. Jonas Bell had been chosen. That's what the man in white, the Phantom of Truth or whoever he was, had said. It began and ended with him. Now he was loose in the world, maybe plotting an encore performance, and the world was a very big place.

Dodger smiled. *No big deal*, he thought. Finding people was his specialty. There was, of course, the matter of what he would do when he finally did track down Bell, but he would cross that bridge when he came to it.

James Pratt lives in southern New Jersey and enjoys writing horror, fantasy, and weird fiction. His influences include H.P. Lovecraft, Jack Vance, Clive Barker, William Hope Hodgson, Clark Ashton Smith, Michael Moorcock, Roger Zelazny, and Stephen King. James's stories have appeared in a number of anthologies including *Canopic Jars: Tales of Mummies and Mummification* from Great Old Ones Press, *Dark Hall Press Cosmic Horror Anthology*, *Alter Egos Vol. 2* from Source Point Press, *Barbarians of the Red Planet* from Rogue Planet Press, *A Mythos Grimmly* from Wanderer's Haven Publications, *Urban Cthulhu* from First United Church of Cthulhu, and *Sunny, With a Chance of Zombies* from KnightWatch Press.

Story illustration by **Aaron White**.

Prisoners of an Invisible Labyrinth

by Joshua Dobson

You know those stories and movies wherein a small isolated town turns out to be peopled entirely by some weird cult? That's how football is around here. On a Friday night during football season a stranger who took a wrong turn somewhere (Which is the only reason I can conceive of as to why a stranger would visit our no horse town; although now that I think about it a stranger did visit our village, and his motive for doing so was far more inscrutable than mere confusion.) as I was saying, the lost stranger would find themselves in a tiny town of deserted streets where the windows of the houses and businesses were all darkened. After sunset the only stoplight in town blinks red, making an electrical sizzling sound that for some reason raises the hairs on the back of one's neck. As the lost stranger wandered the deserted streets, looking for someone to ask for directions back to the highway, the sick sizzling sound would occasionally be drowned out by an electrically amplified voice babbling incomprehensibly while masses of people chanted some phrase he couldn't make out over and over and over again.

The reason I bring this up is to point out that at the height of the furor surrounding the Minotaur, it wasn't to the stadium beside the high school that folks flocked, but rather to the edge of a weed-choked field behind an abandoned building which had once housed a franchise of a retail chain that went out of business decades ago. At one point there was even talk of removing some of the bleachers from the football field and placing them on the edge of the vacant lot. For the Minotaur to outdraw the Fighting Owls is some kind of testament to something or other.

People used to dump trash and broken appliances in that field, some mysterious prankster was in the habit of obscenely posing the dismembered mannequins that had been consigned to the weedy limbo after the nearby store went under, kids would gather there to hump, drink, huff, and smoke in nests of trampled down weeds. This didn't happen after the Minotaur took up residence; people regarded the field with superstitious dread, refusing to set foot in it, as if there was a sea of lava beyond the edge of the cracked concrete of the parking lot where the townsfolk set up the folding lawn chairs in which they sat for hours staring at the Minotaur. It wasn't just people that felt this way. I once saw a mouse scamper across the parking lot towards the weedy field. It stopped at the border, seemingly afraid to leave the pavement. It stuck one paw tentatively across the border, like someone using their toe to gauge the temperature of water in a swimming pool, then the wee rodent rapidly drew back the appendage, raised it to its mouth, and began to gnaw it off.

No one knows from whence the Minotaur came, he was just there one morning, walking through the invisible labyrinth.

I was having breakfast at the diner the fateful morning the preacher burst in, his eyes glistening wildly as they did when he preached his sermon.

"There's some kinda weirdo doing something weird," he said before leading us to the field.

The Minotaur was this tall, gaunt, grey thing. Concentration-camp-skinny, his protruding ribs looked as if they were trying to escape his skin. The ratty beard that dangled almost to his belly was the same shade of grey as his leathery skin. He was completely naked, yet his ancient wrinkled hide never tanned or succumbed to sunburn, his flesh remained subterranean-pale even as it was exposed to the sun all day every day. His feet were bare pilgrims who undertook the trek to the roof of the abandoned store assured those who hadn't.

The weeds hid his feet from the eyes of the crowd in the parking lot, but one day a few intrepid souls used a ladder to climb to the roof of the abandoned store. The pilgrims who undertook the trek assured those of us who hadn't that the Minotaur's bare feet were exceptionally large, perhaps large enough to have left the tracks which were described by the amateur sasquatch hunters who found them in the hills outside town as being reminiscent of one of those floors with dance steps diagrammed on them.

The Minotaur's movements were jerky, like those of a poorly operated marionette. His sclerotic shuffle, according to Doc Kiernan, resembled the motions of someone afflicted with tertiary syphilis.

The Minotaur's ritual had killed the weeds. If you climbed up to the roof of the abandoned store and looked down on the field the pattern which the schizo OCD freak had worn into the weeds, as he endlessly walked the through the invisible maze, rather resembled a crop circle that was discovered in a wheat field outside town one autumn morning a little over twenty years ago.

(And everyone who gazed upon that crop circle, the stories say, found themselves afflicted with the symptoms of a sexually transmitted disease even though tests revealed no pathogens in their systems.)

For many the Minotaur was something they went out of their way not to see. They averted their gaze as they drove past the field and they left the room as soon as talk turned (as all conversations inevitably did) to the subject of the perpetually shambling derelict. But for most of the townsfolk The Minotaur was something they were compelled to look upon.

Nobody was more obsessed with the Minotaur than the first of us to see him. And as his obsession bloomed, the preacher's Sunday sermons grew stranger and stranger. References to God and Jesus were replaced with rants about the Minotaur and convoluted theories that sounded like something one would hear on one of those TV shows where scientifically illiterate charlatans, and/or idiotically deluded true believers, attempt to link various bits of ancient monolithic architecture and strange tribal rites to flying saucers or Deros from inside the hollow earth. The preacher was the first to set up his lawn chair on the edge of the field. Others soon followed and it wasn't long before the parking lot was a sea of chairs.

As they sat in their folding lawn chairs, swilling beer and scarfing down hot dogs while they watched the show, folks theorized about why the derelict trod the maze. Some said he was a schizo, a hardcore obsessive compulsive who believed the world would end, or something even stranger would happen if he didn't walk the labyrinth. Others, including the preacher, said it was some kind of religious thing, like those Mexicans who crawl for miles on their bellies to some obscure mountaintop shrine as a sign of devotion or penance. Some, and I counted myself among them, were of the opinion that he was just a perfectly ordinary bindle-over-shoulder, boxcar-hopping, steal-a-pie-off-a-windowsill hobo who just happened to be passing by when he somehow became trapped inside some kind of sigil scrawled in the field by something from somewhere else. And then there were those who said he was ghost.

He never slept. He must've ate and drank, (unless . . .) but no one had ever seen him perform either of these actions.

And they'd tried to catch him.

It was considered great sport to post up on the edge of the field and watch him for hours. People were determined to catch him eating, drinking, relaxing somehow, but their patience eventually wore thin and they went home while he continued to walk the same path over and over. Some days half the town would be lurking on the edge of the field, sitting in folding lawn chairs, watching this lunatic endlessly clomp through the weeds.

A great many townsfolk became as obsessed with the freak as he seemed to be obsessed with his ritual. People called in sick day after day so they could sit on the edge of the field all day watching him. When they were inevitably fired from their jobs they greeted this news with joy because it gave them more time to watch. Members of the football team missed practices and even games. People had to be reminded to eat and sleep. It's a wonder nobody starved to death in their lawn chair.

The Minotaur was regarded with a mixture of fascination and seething atavistic revulsion, like the displays of pickled punks that used to come through town decades ago, wherein for a small fee one could gaze upon deformed mutant animals (and the occasional human fetus) floating in jars of cloudy fluid.

"Somebody should go tell that freak to stop it. To get the hell outta here," someone said. And everyone agreed but no one wanted to be the one to approach this strange creature.

Even the cops wouldn't go near him.

"He ain't hurtin' nobody," the Sheriff said, lowering his gaze sheepishly as he always did when he was lying.

"But he's trespassing," someone said, as if the Minotaur's presence in the field was somehow causing harm, which it was and everyone knew it was, but nobody could say how or why, and any attempt to articulate the otherworldly sense of wonder and dread awakened by the endlessly shambling derelict would only result in embarrassing them that tried.

"And he's nekkid!" someone said.

"If I was paradin' 'round nekkid as a jaybird you'd lock me up so quick my head would spin!" the Sunday school teacher shouted.

The situation kind of reminded me of that old TV show, *The Addams Family*, like how they were so freakish no one could stand to be around them, even to like collect their taxes, or check their house to make sure it complied with building codes. Like their weirdness put them completely outside the bounds of humanity and its laws.

Sometimes as they sat in their folding lawn chairs staring at the elderly hobo wandering through the invisible labyrinth people would be overwhelmed with rage. They would scream at him, "What the fuck are you doing you goddamn freak? Leave our town alone you crummy bastard." The object of this hatred never gave any indication of having heard anything shouted at him. His shambling steps never faltered. He never raised the eyes that were perpetually focused on his feet.

Sometimes in the grip of rage folks were tempted to throw things at the Minotaur, some would even go so far as to pick up empty beer bottles, rocks, or broken bits of cement from the ground. But they never threw them. They knew that would somehow be even worse than stepping into the field, physical contact with this bizarre freak, even by proxy, was not something one would wish on their worst enemy.

People tried to think of ways to drive him out of the field, like by, for instance, spraying him with a fire hose, or setting the weeds that choked the field on fire. This latter notion, the Scorched Earth Policy as it came to be known, particularly struck a chord and was endlessly discussed though nothing ever came of it.(In no small part because of the fear that it wouldn't do any good, he would continue to walk the maze even as the fire raged around him.)

The only thing more terrifying than the Minotaur's presence was his absence.

Amazingly no one was watching when whatever happened happened, or at least no one will admit as much.

These are the facts: One morning, a little less than a year after he'd appeared in the field, the weeds had been reduced to smoldering ashes, throwing off twisted streams of smoke that climbed into the air to join the stink of burnt flesh that hung above the scorched field. And the Minotaur was nowhere in evidence.

Either a lynch mob carried out the Scorched Earth Policy, or something far stranger occurred in the field that night.

When news of the development spread, the whole town at first sighed with relief, then seconds after the air escaped their lips they felt as if they had somehow been betrayed in some obscure fashion impossible to articulate. As if we had grown addicted to this strange figure and his freakish ritual.

The town sank into depression. In the days following the Minotaur's disappearance there were more suicide attempts than there had been the winter after a fumble cost the Fighting Owls their chance at going to state.

Folks still sat in their lawn chairs, tears streaming from their eyes as they stared at the empty field he'd once roamed.

What transpired over the following weeks was regarded as mass hysteria by some, while others thought it something far stranger.

It started with those who were in the habit of pacing when nervous.

Then folks began to alter the routes they habitually used to get to work or walk through the supermarket (where the mazes on the backs of the cereal boxes seemed to mock us).

The new routes were indirect, elaborate, tangled, doubling back and crossing themselves in loops. Their execution seemed to mean something in and of itself; not merely a path from one point to another, but a sort of performance art.

To get from any one point to any other we first had to walk the Minotaur's path.

It was as if horrible things lurked on either side of us, forcing us through the maze, steering us like cattle being driven down a kill chute.

Some places were forever inaccessible from certain other places because an obstacle such as a wall prevented a crucial turn that had to be undertaken while walking the labyrinth. So, for instance, I found myself unable to walk from my bedroom to the adjoining bathroom without first walking the labyrinth to some place from whence I could walk the labyrinth to the water closet.

During this period it wasn't unusual for someone, whose puzzled and embarrassed countenance showed their mortification, to wander through residences, passing through the parlors and bedrooms of neighbors (or complete strangers) as they attempted to walk from their front porch to the mailbox at the end of their driveway.

Football players would walk the labyrinth on the field in the middle of a game. A promising young wide receiver, who scuttlebutt insisted would surely one day turn pro, died (of "heat exhaustion" the local paper said) after he was pinned under a pile of offensive tackles and prevented from completing the circuit he had been taking through the labyrinth when he was dog-piled.

There were other deaths as well. A young girl fell down a well, while "sleepwalking" as the local paper put it; but we knew. Some people's path through the labyrinth took them across streets full of speeding traffic.(In these instances it was better when they died. The sight of someone with broken legs desperate to complete the labyrinth dragging themselves along the ground with their arms was just too much to take.)

In the early stages, when the compulsion to traverse the maze only attached itself to pedestrianism it was chaotic, but once people began to feel the call of the labyrinth while driving it became nigh on apocalyptic. Cars would suddenly veer off streets, slamming into walls, driving off bridges, mowing over pedestrians, plummeting off cliffs.

Those of us who gathered on the edge of the field one crisp autumn morning, a few months after the Minotaur disappeared, knew what needed to be done. No words were spoken. We looked at one another and knew that each of us was thinking the same thing. The maze had escaped the field when the Minotaur vanished. One of us must be imprisoned in the labyrinth so that the others might be free of it.

We drew straws.(Never has there been a sweeter sight than the hearty length of the straw I plucked from the mayor's hand.)

The preacher, the very same fellow who'd been the first to discover the ancient derelict shambling through the invisible labyrinth in the weed-choked field, drew the short straw. The preacher was also one of them who were present in their lawn chairs when the previous Minotaur met his fate (and whatever he saw that night had turned his fiery red hair as white as the face of death.).He knows the fate that awaits him in the heart of the labyrinth.

"Go Fightin' Owls!" the preacher said, before he stripped off his clothes, walked up to the border, hesitated, then trudged into the field (his movements growing more and more jerky and puppet-like the closer he progressed to the ruts worn into the ground.)As he began to traverse the invisible maze, the rest of us settled into our lawn chairs and sighed in relief, feeling as if a great weight had been lifted.

Joshua Dobson is the pseudonym of a brood of mutant jellyfish that achieved sentience after drifting through a cloud of toxic waste and now devotes its hive mind to dreading hungry sea turtles, writing short fiction, and eagerly awaiting the day when the ice caps melt. http://joshuadobson.deviantart.com/

Story illustration by **Sean O'Keefe**.

FROM
LOVECRAFT EZINE PRESS

The Endless Fall, by Jeffrey Thomas

Whispers, by Kristin Dearborn

Nightmare's Disciple, by Joseph S. Pulver, Sr.

Autumn Cthulhu, edited by Mike Davis

The Lurking Chronology, by Pete Rawlik

The Sea of Ash, by Scott Thomas

The King in Yellow Tales volume I, by Joseph S. Pulver, Sr.

Blood Will Have Its Season, by Joseph S. Pulver, Sr.

www.ingramcontent.com/pod-product-compliance
Lightning Source LLC
Chambersburg PA
CBHW030611130626
46552CB00002B/514